Proudly
They
Serve

Clifton LaBree

© 2015 by Fading Shadows Imprint

Published by
Fading Shadows Imprint
New Boston, New Hampshire, USA

Paperback ISBN-13: 978-1-943329-29-8

Cover Image Northland WMEC 904:
https://commons.wikimedia.org/wiki/
File:USCGC_Northland_WMEC-904.jpg
USCGC Northland WMEC-904 bow view.
Date: Unknown
Source:
www.uscg.mil/lantarea/cutter/northland/Images/904_BOW.JPG
www.uscg.mil/lantarea/cutter/northland/facts.htm
Author: USCG

This book is a work of fiction. The characters are fictional, but the historical events and dates have been seriously researched and are factually presented. Any resemblance to actual persons is entirely coincidental.

Dedicated to my wife Pauline, and my family, with thanks for all their support and encouragement

Chapter One

Nathan Collins sat on the cliffs overlooking the churning Atlantic restlessly assaulting the jagged shore. He was intimately familiar with the varied moods of the sea, having served nearly twenty years as a chief petty officer in the United States Coast Guard, primarily in the Atlantic. He had a taciturn demeanor most of the time, yet his friends saw him smile often. It was his deep-set eyes that caught most people's attention. They reflected the turmoil and horror that had been a large part of his adult life. Nothing came easy for him. Every effort seemed to be an uphill struggle.

He remembered with distinct clarity how it had been soon after he had joined the Coast Guard. The Great Depression had affected every family in the land. Times were difficult. Jobs were scarce, and money was even scarcer. His father had been a machinist on one of the ferries that ran from Belfast to several of the islands off the coast of Maine. The family was thankful that the ferries continued to run even after the depression reached its lowest point.

When Nathan graduated from Belfast High School he could not find a job anywhere. Unsure of what he wanted to do in life, Nathan declined an offer to attend college and decided to join the Coast Guard the summer of 1935. The steady paycheck would allow him to save for the day when he and Shirley Mason could marry. Three years later, they married after he had been promoted to petty officer first class with two stripes.

The world was in great turmoil. Japan was busy enlarging its sphere of influence by taking control of China, Malaya, the Philippines, and several smaller islands in the Pacific on their way to Australia. On the other side of the world, Germany's armies were smashing their way to victories involving much of Europe with little resistance. The world was on fire, and the United States was woefully unprepared to counter those unleashed forces of evil even to defend themselves. The future looked grim.

Canada and England had called for assistance in transporting the life-sustaining supplies across the North Atlantic to England. The United States was bound by custom, common law, and speech to do what we could to assist. At that time, the United States was a neutral nation, yet we escorted several convoys of badly needed supplies to our friends well before war was declared.

The dark boiling waters of the North Atlantic were treacherous enough without having to worry about lurking German submarines that had found bountiful hunting grounds against the convoys. Hundreds of ships were sunk by their deadly torpedoes. The Germans usually attacked with several submarines at the same time much like wolves attacking a deer. The wolf pack tactic was most successful, allowing the Germans to sink more ships than were being constructed in either England or the United States. If that situation continued, Germany could effectively defeat the British without invading their homeland.

It was a depressing state of affairs, and those who served in the convoys did so in constant fear of the silent death threat that lurked beneath the waters. Death could come at any time, day or night, without warning. Sailors lived with the terror and grew old before their time, yet, they continued to man the precious lifeline from the U.S. to England and later to Russia.

War material was sent to England under the Lend-Lease Program, allowing them to pay for the material at a later date or return it. It was an unprecedented act of generosity between nations.

The first United States force to respond to the British and Canadian request were Coast Guard high endurance cutters which had been utilized for years in the North Atlantic. The cutters were approximately two hundred seventy feet long with a crew of one hundred men. Heavily armed and very seaworthy, the gunboats were light with a shallow draft making them extremely uncomfortable in heavy seas. They had a cruising range of about nine thousand miles. The traditional missions of the Coast Guard in the North Atlantic included maintaining navigational aids, assisting any ship in need of assistance regardless of nationality, weather data collection and reporting, fisheries inspection, and iceberg mapping patrols.

The cutters were equipped with depth charges, sonar, and adequate gunnery to challenge the German submarine (U-boat) threat. The Coast Guard dispatched a large number of its cutter fleet to escort duty. Once the maneuverable ships arrived, losses to submarines were less. Frequently the valiant cutters were placed beside valuable cargo ships in the direct line of attack. Those who experienced the dedication and professionalism of the Coast Guard ships were impressed.

Nathan served for much of the duration of the war on the *Northland* cutter. The crew had sunk two U-boats prior to the time when war was declared. The crew was as tenacious in combat as they were compassionate in their role as lifesavers at sea. He always took comfort from the delicate balancing between the two missions that the force was famous for. The fact that they viewed their lifesaving role as primary placed them in a unique category, distinct from the other armed forces. In peacetime they were the only force with arrest powers. Their interaction with the general public was much greater than the Army or Navy. That made the Coasties a little more socially conscious, creating a softer imprint on the general public. This generated a great deal of goodwill among the people. Their dedication to serving the country had few equals.

Nathan's patrols in the North Atlantic were sometimes frightening and often beautiful. He eventually developed an affection for the arctic region. When the sun disappeared for weeks at a time, an eerie twilight, halfway between day and night, enveloped the region. It generated different emotions in people. It reminded Nathan of a phrase used in an article by Ernie Pyle, a beloved American journalist, to describe how bomber crews felt flying over Germany: "It was just that on some nights, the air became sick, and there was an unspoken contagion of spiritual dread, and we were little boys again lost in the dark."

The deep, dark water of the North Atlantic was the burial place for thousands of sailors who braved the relentless efforts of German pilots and submariners to destroy them and their charges of defenseless transports carrying the lifeblood of resistance to the Russians and the English. Any seaman that went into the water had only about two minutes to survive its frigid temperatures. Rescue efforts were rarely successful. The Atlantic claimed its victims with stunning efficiency!

One trip, early in the war of the North Atlantic, Nathan recalled a tall, thin North Dakota farmer, Norman "Slim" Kelly. Slim had taken the attacks by the Germans personally. He was the gunner on the port fifty-caliber machine gun turret next to the bridge. The Captain was warned that a flight of German bombers and fighters from occupied Norway were heading for the convoy and had ordered everyone to battle stations. Slim was secured in the turret when a twin-engine German Dornier began a sweep of the cutter, front to stern. Slim immediately saw the threat and began firing both guns into the oncoming bomber. The brave Slim Kelly never once released his fingers from the triggers of his guns. He peppered the aircraft turning the gun barrels a cherry red. The amount of damage he did to the aircraft, was unknown. He was almost cut in two by the twenty mm cannons on the plane. Death came quickly to the young gunner.

Nathan had been busy directing the fire of automatic Swedish Bofor anti-aircraft guns during the attack. Slim Kelly was slumped over his turret, bleeding profusely. Nathan had closed his eyelids and helped to remove his battered body from the turret. He could still see the horror that registered in Slim's eyes. Nathan had the sad duty to write a letter to Slim's family, notifying them of his death and burial at sea. It was the first casualty in his company, and he never forgot it.

Sometimes the numerous patrols got all mixed up in his mind. It was easy to lose track of time. Each one had its unique horror tale to recall. On one of the runs to Murmansk, Nathan remembered seeing a large freighter cut in half by a torpedo. Most of the load was Studebaker ten-wheel trucks destined for the Russian Army. The trucks began to slide out of both halves of the freighter into the deep water of the Atlantic. His family had been Studebaker enthusiasts for years. He thought it was a shame to waste such fine engineering in such an ignoble manner.

Deck watches became a long, lonely vigil with a very real danger of being tossed overboard. The small cutters, fully equipped for convoy escort duty, rocked and pitched like a bucking bronco. The movement never stopped. At times it was impossible to hold a plate of food or a cup of coffee on the mess table. Sleep became an ordeal. The small bunks for the enlisted men held them captive. Every man got bumps and bruises from the sides of their bunks. That did not cultivate restful sleep. Watches on the bridge near the epicenter of the vessel were the easiest to endure.

Walking on the walls was not uncommon. Green recruits laughed at the phrase until they experienced it for the first time. They often turned a pale green around the eyes and nose and retched more often than seasoned sailors. No one was immune to the ordeal. A patrol in the North Atlantic frequently was an exercise in terror unequalled in any other war zone.   Nathan mentally reviewed major events in his life with anger and sadness. The most traumatic incident took place the day he had returned to port in Boston after a round trip escorting a supply ship convoy to and from England. He remembered that homecoming with great clarity. He rushed ashore to call home. There was no answer from the phone at the apartment he and Shirley had rented in Belfast, Maine. He tried again and got the same message — the number was no longer in service. Fear that something horrible had happened to his wife and son of six months frightened him. Filled with dread, he called his parent's home. His mother answered the phone.

"Hello."

"Ma!" he cried. "Where's Shirley and little Casey? I tried the phone, but it's not working. Has anything happened to them?" Horrible thoughts ran through his mind.

"We've been waiting for your call, son. Now you've got to be strong, Nat. There's no easy way to tell you that Shirley has left town with a pilot friend. We were aware for some time that she was seeing someone…"

"You mean she just left, just like that?" he hollered into the receiver. "She left without a word to me? What about Casey?"

His mother tried to calm him. "She left a note with us that she wanted a divorce. We had been caring for Casey for a few days. He's still with us and is doing just fine. We had no way of getting in touch with you. The Coast Guard could not confirm where you could be contacted. I know how hard this must be for you, son. Your dad and I have been worried sick about this sudden turn of events. I must tell you that she was never the girl you thought she was. We saw things you didn't, and we did not want to hurt you…"

"What am I going to do about Casey, Ma?"

"Can you come home for awhile?"

"Yes, that's why I'm calling. I'll catch a bus and get there as quickly as I can. I've got a few days leave before the *Northland* is ready for another patrol." He had a hard time containing the tears struggling for release.

"We understand how difficult this is for you, son, but in the long run, you're better off without her. She was no good for you or for little Casey. Your steady paycheck from the Coast Guard was a big attraction for her. Are you all right, son?" his mother asked, concerned for his emotional state of mind.

"I don't know how to answer that, Mom. I was looking forward to a reunion with them for a few days. It hurts a lot, Ma, but don't worry for me. I'll be home soon. Thank God you and Pa are there for Casey."

That furlough had been the saddest of his long career. He never got any logical explanation from Shirley for her actions.

Her abandonment of Casey was evidently done without regret. These two dastardly acts had left him with an overpowering hatred for her and everything she represented... He became a bitter man. His wife had failed him when he needed her the most, and she was well aware of that desperate need.

Chapter Two

Wells Beach, Maine, Summer 1951

Twenty years of experience in the Coast Guard had taken him to Alaska for one year in 1948 and to Korea in 1950 for almost two years. The balance of his service time was spent in the North Atlantic aboard several Coast Guard vessels, primarily high endurance cutters.

All of his years were memorable and had left their mark on him, but his short stay at the very beginning of the war at Wells, Maine where he had set up coastal patrols and manned an observation tower, was recalled with strong emotional feelings he was never able to control. He felt a need to return to the scene of that period to sort out those feelings that had always been dormant beneath his consciousness that early in his career. The defection of his wife; the birth of his son; his baptism to combat; and the ensuing losses of several of his men from gunfire had matured him beyond his years. From that moment on, he was in constant search of peace of mind, never sure just how that might be accomplished. He had found a level of comfort and stability for a short period of time in the small community of Wells.

Watching the rocky shore in front of the now abandoned cement observation tower, Nathan's heart pounded just thinking of that magic time in his youth. Warm memories flooded through him as he returned to those eventful days in the fall of 1941 prior to the attack on Pearl Harbor by the Japanese.

Nathan had unofficially been at war for a year and a half in the North Atlantic, escorting desperately needed supplies to

England. German submarines and attack bombers were a deadly menace the moment the convoys gathered off the coast of the United States until they arrived in England. The route from the eastern coast to Halifax or St. Johns in Canada was paved with the sunken hulls of freighters who succumbed to the deadly threat lurking beneath the dark waters of the North Atlantic. Thousands of brave seamen's spirits, remaining forever young, still haunt the hazardous supply route.

In the summer of 1941, one convoy had braved most of the vicious North Atlantic, losing three ships to torpedo attacks and were entering the western approaches to the British Isles. It was the area where German aircraft were able to reach the convoys from their captured bases in northern Norway. On this particular trip, the weather was clear and sunny, perfect weather for the planes! Every captain in the convoy knew that the area they had just entered was the most dangerous stretch of all. Their fears were soon realized as the sky was filled with German bombers and fighters.

They lost more than ten vessels to the bombers. Nathan's cutter was in the middle of the engagement with every available gun blazing at the tenacious German fliers. They were aided by the submarines who accounted for some of the losses on that voyage. He was busy directing the twin mounts of the 20 mm Swedish Bofor anti-aircraft guns when a bomber made a full run against the cutter from stem to stern, peppering the ship with heavy cannon fire.

Several Coasties were killed in the intense engagement, and many were wounded, including Nathan. He was hit by a ragged piece of shrapnel that entered his lower abdomen near his hip joint. Several smaller red-hot pieces of molten metal covered the left side of his body. All of the wounds bled profusely, leaving him weak and unconscious for the duration of the German attack. He fought tenaciously against being placed in a British hospital, insisting that the ship's pharmacist mate could treat the wounds until they returned to the states. His Captain agreed with his decision, insisting that Nathan remain in his bunk until they arrived at a port in the United States. The home port of the cutter *Response* was Portsmouth, New Hampshire Naval Shipyard.

He was transferred to the base hospital where his wounds were properly treated. He was relieved to learn that his largest wound would not limit him in any way after it had healed. He was one of the lucky ones. Several days later, he was visited by the regional Coast Guard commander, Lieutenant Commander Judd Schultz. Nathan was half asleep on his hospital bed listening to the sounds of the Navy Yard. The desperate need of submarines by the Navy was pushing the manufacturing process at a rapid tempo. He was listening to a symphony of noises that would eventually result in another submarine.

He did not see the Commander enter his ward until he was standing beside his bed. "I hope that my visit has not interrupted your rest, Collins,"

Nathan replied, "Not at all, Commander. The people here at Kittery have been swell. There's a chair next to my stand if you'd like to sit for a while."

Commander Schultz placed the chair so that Nathan could see him easily. "I wanted to talk with you about a few things, Chief. First, how are your wounds coming along?"

"They're doing fine, Sir. The new antibiotic medicine, penicillin, works wonders. I'm mending from the ordeal."

"I'm glad to hear that." The Commander reached into his tunic inside pocket to pull out an envelope. "I'm pleased to announce your promotion to Chief Petty Officer. This letter contains the orders, and I've requested the Navy here on the base to supply you with all of the proper and necessary clothing that goes with the rate. We're all proud of your service. Your dedication to duty and efficiency have earned the promotion. As you well know, the chiefs of the Coast Guard and Navy run the shows. Officers are helpless without the performance of the chiefs who make the wheels turn. Congratulations, Chief Collins."

The promotion was unexpected. He took the envelope. "Thank you, Sir. I'll do my best to be worthy of the rank."

"I'm sure you will, Chief. I've taken the liberty of supplying you with your new hat insignia and chevrons. I joined the Coast Guard as a young man. These insignias have been lucky for me. I hope they do the same for you."

"It will be an honor to wear them, Commander. Your reputation in the Coast Guard will be a guiding example for me. Thanks. I really appreciate your support."

Commander Schultz looked at him with a serious frown. "Chief, I want to talk to you about a project that needs to be done. As you must know, our country is at risk right now. The politicians have let us down. The Army and Navy are scrambling to make up for lost time. The consensus of most military leaders is that we'll be at war with Japan and Germany within the year. I tell you this because I'm going to ask you for a personal favor. Normally, I'd insist that you take a well-deserved furlough with your family."

Nathan was impressed with the concerned look on his commander's face. "What do you want me to do, Sir?"

"I'm not ordering you, Chief. I'm asking you to volunteer for a task the Coast Guard has been given to secure our coastlines. We've already built several coastal observation towers on the Atlantic seaboard. One is in Wells, Maine, just a few miles from here. I'd like for you to organize the security patrols for the Wells district just as soon as the doctors give you the clearance to return to limited duty. I've already assigned a roster of twenty men to the post. We've secured a large house and barn capable of housing the men and materials."

Nathan listened to the Commander's description of the task. "I'd be glad to take on the project, Sir. It'll be a welcome break from escort duty. I just heard that the Coast Guard will be getting several of the Navy's four-stack destroyers for duty in the North Atlantic. They'll be a much more comfortable ship than the lighter and shorter cutters. I've been in the Coast Guard long enough to realize that they grant more authority to enlisted ranks than any of the other services. I'll be glad to give this new position my best effort, but I'm surprised that you don't place an officer in charge."

"You raise a valid point, Chief. The answer is we don't have enough officers available. We're expanding our number of ships and are taking responsibility for manning several hundred of the Army's ships, large and small. I would not have suggested this job if I felt you were not up to the task."

"I'm flattered, Sir. Just as soon as I'm able to move about without assistance, I'll move into the new quarters."

Commander Schultz stood up to leave. "I'll see to it that you get one of the Coast Guard's best clerks, Chief. He'll be given the men's files and every authorization you may need to carry out your duties. "I've got to run, Chief. Best of luck to you. I hope your recovery is swift and complete. The house and tower will have whatever you need."

"I look forward to the challenge, Commander Schultz. Maybe I could have my folks bring my son to Wells for a visit," Nathan mused.

The Commander turned at the door to look at him. "I would not object if you turned one of the rooms in the house into a hospitality room for visiting guests. Short visits from your family would be acceptable, but I'd frown on lengthy stays at the facility. Do you understand?"

"I read you loud and clear, Sir."

The Portsmouth Navy Yard doctors had insisted that he stay at the facility for several days after his promotion. The wound had penetrated deep into his body against his joint and they were concerned about internal infection. Two days after Commander Schultz left, Nathan had a visitor.

"Chief Collins, I'm Seaman Second Class Jim Reams. Commander Schultz has ordered me to be your company clerk."

Nathan was not surprised to learn that things were happening rapidly. Jim Reams was a short, compact young man with broad shoulders slightly younger than Nathan. He had a round face and smiled often. His quiet demeanor and confident body language generated trust. Nathan was quick to like the man. He mentally told himself that the Commander had lived up to his word. Over the period of his stay at Wells, Reams became his indispensable assistant.

"What kind of a situation are we getting into, Jim?"

"Well, I've just come from Wells. The house and attached barn are perfect for the operation. We can have everything under one roof. Right now the Army engineers are busy converting two rooms into a dining hall and food serving facility. They've already completed renovating the attic and cellar into adequate rooms to house the company. I think we'll be comfortable. The Army will be responsible for coastal security on both sides of Wells. Our territory extends north along the coast to Drake's Island, south to Ogunquit. Most of our supplies will be coming from the Army."

"That sounds great, Jim. When will the house be available for occupancy?" Nathan asked.

"The Army engineers told me they needed two more days. We're going to use the old .03 Springfield rifle. The new Garand M-1 is only being issued to the Army's expeditionary troops," Jim told him.

"Oh well. Both rifles use the same ammo," Nathan sighed. "We'll make do with what we have. That's a tradition in the Coast Guard. Have you gone over the roster of men yet?"

"Most are young men fresh out of boot camp. They won't be receiving orders until you're well enough to take up residence at the post. I'm going to be your company clerk and your assistant, Chief Collins. I hope that things work out for us. I'm prepared to give you my best."

"I could not ask for better, Jim. Tell the commander that I'm just as anxious to get out of this hospital as he is to activate the post at Wells."

Later that same day, Nathan was surprised to see his mother and father walk into his ward at the hospital. His father was holding his one-year-old son, Casey, in his strong arms. They all embraced each other. His mother broke out in tears when she saw all of the bandages he had wrapped around his body.

"Don't cry, Ma. My wounds are not as bad as they appear. It's nice to see you two. I've missed you a lot."

Henry Collins placed Casey on the pillow beside Nathan's head. "This little runt is your son. He's a strong, spry little fellow."

Nathan turned to look into his son's eyes. Little Casey was sucking on a pacifier eyeing the stranger near him. "He has Shirley's eyes and nose. Hello, little man. I'm your Daddy." Nat held his tiny hand. Casey wrapped his hand around his father's thumb and squeezed it.

This precious little human being triggered a shower of emotions Nathan had been holding inside since his mother told him about Shirley's disappearance. Tears began to roll out of the corner of his eyes down into his neck and onto his shoulders. His parents looked upon his mounting grief with feelings of helplessness. His wife had abandoned him with impunity, administering an emotional upheaval he little deserved. What could they say or do except to be there for their only son? This was the first time that he really faced the stark truth of what had happened to his marriage. The catharsis, though hurtful for his parents to witness, had a cleansing effect that surprised him. For some reason, the response triggered a determination to go forward and never look back.

The short visit of his parents gave him a clearer view of the road he must take for the future. They successfully convinced him that Casey was definitely not a burden to them. It was almost as if they were reliving Nathan's childhood. Their desire to give his son a caring and giving home helped him to answer the question: "Where do I go from here?" For now, there was no viable course available to him.

They talked about old friends and happenings in town since Nat left for the Coast Guard. Everybody was filled with uncertainty about the encroaching winds of war. They cautioned Nathan to take good care of himself and not to worry about Casey. They had the home front well covered. He never loved his parents as much as he had on that day when the world was poised for disaster. Little did they know just how destructive it would become…

Nathan received a letter from Shirley on the same day he was scheduled to leave the hospital for Wells:

Dear Nathan,

My guilty heart will not allow me to remain silent any longer. My sudden betrayal of our marriage vows and Casey has turned my world upside down. Sitting here now with pen in hand I'd handle the situation differently if I had it to do over again. But, alas, one can't turn back the clock…

My reason for leaving is that I love another man more than I love you, Nathan. I know that statement hurts, but it's the truth. Your long absences from home were just too much for my insecure and immature character to handle.

I beg you to understand my feelings if you can. It would have been wrong to have stayed together. I never should have married. I thought the financial security was important, but it was not enough.

I don't blame you for hating me. I'm sorry that I've caused you so much grief. I'll pray for you and Casey.

Good-bye,

Shirley

Even now, ten years later, Nathan could feel the same trauma that letter had inflicted on him. Her betrayal was a harsh reality for him to swallow. At the same time, he looked upon the new duty station with pride and a deep sense of loneliness. October 1941 and the months that followed were etched on his memory. How could he ever forget?

Chapter Three

The doctor at the Portsmouth Navy Yard Hospital authorized Nathan to assume light duties at the Wells facility with the understanding that he would avoid activities that were too physical. He was pleased to leave the hospital with Jim Reams in a Dodge military truck that had been assigned to the Wells detachment.

The Army engineers had completed their work on the house and barn shortly before the twenty-man company arrived from Boston. The house was capable of berthing the whole detachment with a hospitality room for guests and a small private room that was converted to an infirmary equipped with basic hygiene and medical supplies. Jim and Nathan shared a private room off the headquarters reception center, with the large dining room adjacent to the main entrance.

The new men checked their assigned living quarters and the four-story cement observation tower across the road from their barracks. The tower was built on the highest point of elevation with a panoramic view of the Atlantic Ocean. It was equipped with a powerful telescope capable of defining any object on the horizon. It was fixed on a calibrated directional finder very similar to that found in most lookout towers for forest fires. When a vessel was located by the Wells tower, and by any other tower on the coast such as at the Nubble Lighthouse in York, the object could be triangulated, giving its precise position.

16

Nathan was dressed for the first time in his newly tailored chief's uniform. When they arrived at Wells, Jim called the men together to introduce their new chief. They lined up in two rows of ten each. All of the men were recent recruits fresh out of boot training, between the ages of seventeen and twenty. How young and innocent they looked to his battle-seasoned eyes. Aside from their youthfulness, he saw that pride and dedication that was such a prominent part of every Coastie. The Coast Guard cultivated a deep sense of service and commitment in its members with the expectation that those values would always be honored. He felt old in comparison. The fact that he was using a cane and his chest displayed several rows of campaign ribbons instantly won their respect.

Nathan saluted the men and ordered them to stand easy. "Men, I'm Chief Petty Officer Nathan Collins, commander of the Wells station. This is Second Class Petty Officer Jim Reams, my assistant and second in command. This is the first time we've met. In time I'll get to know all of you by name. I want to start out by telling you what I expect from every one of you. For the next few days my wound will keep me close to the headquarters building. As I improve, I'll be out on the patrols with you. I'm not an officer, so we can dispense with some of the formalities of a military formation. That's not the same as abandoning all normal courtesies and customs. I'm responsible for everything that takes place at this station; consequently, things are going to be done my way. I might make some mistakes along the way, and I'm expecting you to bring them to my attention. If you keep me from making an ass of myself, I'll be eternally grateful to you.

"I'm always available to discuss any problem, personal or otherwise, in private. My door is never locked. Remember, we are Coasties, and we have a tradition of excellence that will be upheld by this detachment at Wells. I have a few thoughts about your interaction with the good people here at Wells. Courtesy and respect will always be the orders of the day. We are here to serve. If you fail me in that department you'll find that my wrath is most unpleasant, and never forget that I sign your fitness reports. My final word is that I want this detachment to always present themselves in a good light. The Coast Guard has a depth of goodwill with the civilian population. Be proud to build upon that respect and pride. When you conduct yourselves in that manner, you'll find me your biggest supporter. Thanks. Now you can return to getting settled into your new quarters."

The station had a full-time cook and a baker. The enlisted men were to assist with kitchen duties on a rotational basis. There was no pharmacist mate assigned to them. Instead, the regional command had arranged for the local doctor at Wells to provide medical care as needed. Their infirmary room was available for minor illnesses. The men went on six-hour shifts which took place at noon and midnight and at six in the morning and evening. Two men were constantly on duty at the tower. Nine men per shift were dispersed on patrol along the coast at a distance of about a half mile. Each post checked into the tower every two hours.

It took about a week to fine-tune the routines. Jim did an excellent job of handling that task for Nathan. The Dodge truck was used to post the sentries and retrieve them. It was kept available at the tower for immediate use. The Navy delivered a Jeep to the station which Nathan used. It had a thirty caliber machinegun mount between the two front seats. It did not take long for the Coasties at Wells to realize that they had drawn a winner in their choice of cook and baker. The food was outstanding. Nathan was especially happy about that. He knew that good food contributed substantially to good morale. He made it a point to congratulate the cook and baker. Coffee, sandwiches, and some form of pastry was always available around the clock. The Coast Guard, like the Navy, thrived on coffee.

Several days after taking control of the Wells station Nathan began to feel weak and felt feverish. Jim called Doctor Colleen Mackey, the local physician, to check him out. He was concerned for his chief. Dr. Mackey pulled into the headquarters building in a Nash Ambassador five-passenger coupe and entered the building. Jim met her at the door.

"Hello, I'm Dr. Mackey," she announced herself to Jim.

Jim shook her hand surprised to see a female doctor. "I'm glad to meet you, Dr. Mackey. I'm the one who called for you.

Our chief, Nathan Collins, was wounded on one of his patrols in the North Atlantic. He was treated at the Portsmouth Navy Yard Hospital. I think he's been overdoing it. Come, please follow me."

Nathan had fallen asleep. Jim gently spoke in his ear. "Chief, I've called the doctor for you."

He stirred, saw the woman in his room, and did not make the connection that she was the doctor. "I'm Doctor Mackey, Chief Collins. Are you surprised to see a woman doctor?"

"I didn't think I needed a doctor," he replied, giving Jim a questioning look. "I was just more tired than usual. I'm pleased to meet you, Dr. Mackey. I've been meaning to speak to you about your services to the station."

She smiled. "Well, here I am. Your assistant was worried about you and it looks to me as if you're running a fever." She placed a hand on his forehead. It was hotter than normal. "May I take a look at your wound, Chief? When was the last time your wound was dressed?"

She removed her long coat. Jim placed it on a coat rack. Nathan was embarrassed pulling down his pants to expose the wound.

"Don't worry, Chief. The male anatomy is no secret to me. You're running a fever."

Jim answered her question. "I changed the dressing for the Chief last night. If you need me, I'll be in the next room."

"Thank you," she said, carefully examining the still draining open wound. It had become infected with red inflamed tissue. "You should have called me sooner. I'm going to wash it with hydrogen peroxide. You need penicillin to fight the infection, Chief."

She pulled a small table close to her side, asking Jim for a supply of clean towels, and exposed the whole wound. It was boiling with white froth from the hydrogen peroxide, indicating that infection had spread to all of the injury. Jim handed her some towels, and winced at the site of the infection. She placed the towels under Nathan so that the draining wound would not soil the sheets on the bed.

She began to roll up his right sleeve. "I'm going to give you an injection of penicillin in your arm. Do you object?"

He looked at her with an amused smile. "Would it do any good if I did object?"

She laughed easily, "I guess not, Chief."

She gently cleaned the wound and gave it one more treatment with liberal amounts of hydrogen peroxide. After cleaning it a second time, she coated the wound with a yellow sulfur powder.

"Do you have any more of the large dressing pads the hospital used?"

"Yes, we do, Dr. Mackey. I'll get them," Jim volunteered again.

She completed dressing the wound and placed a thermometer in his mouth. She had a gentle way about her. Nathan watched her collect things into her black bag. She had auburn hair done up in a bun at the back of her head. She had a few small freckles near the tip of her nose. There was a confident air that made people feel comfortable with her. She carried herself erect and proud. By traditional standards she was not beautiful, but she did have that illusive quality of strength and dignity. She was comfortable and at ease with who she was. Most people found that reassuring. Her strong presence inherently made people notice her, yet she was not a show-off.

"Your temperature is 101 degrees. You should drink as much liquid as you can handle, Chief Collins. The wound will take some time to heal. I'd like to look at it again tomorrow. In the meantime, try to rest. Is there anything else I may help you with?" she asked, reaching for her coat on the rack.

"How do we handle your fees, Doctor?" Nathan asked.

"I'll bill the district command at Boston directly. They're the ones who contacted me about supplying you with medical attention as needed. I'm the only doctor in town. If you have a situation where you need assistance beyond a home visit, go directly to the Navy Yard Hospital at Portsmouth. Of course, I'll come anytime I'm called. I came here two years ago directly from my internship at Mass General in Boston."

"I'd say that the Regional Headquarters made a wise choice, Dr. Mackey. The town is well served. Thank you for coming," Nathan told her.

"It's my pleasure, Chief. The town is excited about your presence here. The world is about to explode and anxiety over the future touches every family. People sleep better just knowing that you're here. We thank you for coming, Chief." She pronounced each word distinctly in a soft, melodious voice. It was a reflection of the peace that radiated from her.

"It's nice to be appreciated, Doctor," he answered, watching her put on her coat. She was a fascinating woman. He reflected that one could know her for a long time and still discover new things about her.

"What time is best for you tomorrow?"

"I think my assistant will keep me captive until you arrive," Nathan smiled. "Any time that fits your schedule will be fine."

"I try to make my house calls in the afternoon, but sometimes emergencies interfere. Good-bye, Chief. Rest well."

Jim escorted her to the Nash and opened the door for her. "I have an uncle who's a doctor in rural Pennsylvania. I can appreciate what it took for a lady to penetrate what has traditionally been a good-old-boys' club. Congratulations, Dr. Mackey. Your patients are the beneficiaries of your successful determination."

"Thank you, Seaman Reams. It was easier than you think, but thanks just the same."

The next day Jim took the responsibility of inserting the men on their stations. Early that evening at dusk, two rubber boats with two men in each came ashore in a high tide at the sandy beach section in front of the Wells Beach pavilion. The minute they climbed out of the boats, lights blinded them, and they were ordered to raise their hands. The Coast Guard patrol had picked them up with their powerful binoculars an hour earlier, remaining out of sight until the crafts touched shore. As it turned out, the four men in the two rubber boats were Coasties ordered to test the effectiveness of the Wells patrol.

Commander Schultz sent a "well done" message to the detachment. The evening meal was a celebration of their success. Nathan had remained in bed most of the day reviewing inventory records and preparing daily logs. When Jim told him about the test, he put on a bathrobe and walked to the dining room.

"I wanted to congratulate you men for doing your job. However, I want to warn against complacency. If a real enemy was determined to enter our country for whatever reason, he would do so at night when we are still blind in many areas. I'm proud of you, but don't take it too far." He smiled and sat down to have a bowl of chicken soup. They had chicken the night before which provided the basics for a hearty soup stock. Their cook was resourceful.

Dr. Mackey pulled up to the station just as Nathan was served his soup. Jim saw her get out of her Ambassador and invited her inside for something to eat. There was a bite to the air and a hot bowl of soup would taste good. She took a seat beside Nathan who told her what had happened at the casino.

She replied, "Well, I heard a similar version at the drug store at Wells Corner. The rumor is that you captured some enemy agents who resisted arrest. You know how gossip can travel in a small town? Nothing is sacred," she laughed softly.

The steward served her the soup. Nathan stood up to address the men in the room. "Men, I want to introduce Dr. Mackey to you. She is a local doctor and has agreed to serve us at the station with medical services as needed. I want all of you to extend a helping hand to the lady. We're fortunate to have her on call. Carry on."

She pushed her chair back and stood to face the young Coasties. "Your Chief has been kind. I will give you my best because I know that you are giving us yours. We really appreciate your dedication and sacrifice on our behalf. You men in uniform represent the best this country has to offer. I speak from experience. My husband is in the Army in the Philippines serving under General MacArthur. Thank you all for your kind hospitality."

While Nathan, Jim, and Dr. Mackey were eating their soup, the contingent of Coasties introduced themselves to Dr. Mackey and left the room. They were a small group of typical young Americans prepared to risk their lives for their country. Nathan was proud of them. The Doctor was right; they are the best. Loyal, kind, and courteous, they were compassionate and caring young men when the situation required empathy. They could also be tenacious warriors defending their loved ones and their homeland.

After the soup, they had hot apple pie and a cup of coffee. Nathan led the way back to his room where the Doctor cleaned and dressed his wound again. It was beginning to heal, and she continued with another dose of penicillin to insure healing.

"Compared to yesterday, your wound looks much better, Chief. I'll check your temperature for the record." She placed a thermometer in his mouth for a minute and checked it. "It's as I thought, normal. You're the kind of patient that makes a doctor feel good. Just continue to go easy for a few more days. You'll be back to normal in no time."

"There's so much to do. If Jim keeps on handling things so efficiently I could be out of a job," he grinned.

"I expect his efficiency is a tribute to the standards you set, Chief."

"Is your husband a doctor?" Nathan asked.

"Yes. He had joined the Maine National Guard right out of high school and remained active through his years of college. The money helped a lot. The battalion was activated, and he went with them as a doctor in the Army Medical Corps. First they went to San Francisco before being shipped to the Philippines. MacArthur is asking for more men and supplies."

Nathan could see that she was concerned about the situation. "I've heard the same thing. The Navy is having trouble sending ships and men to the two ocean fronts. I certainly don't want to add to your concern, but your husband's location at the extreme limit of our resources will probably become our first line of resistance if the Japanese continue with their bold moves across the Pacific. God willing, it will not take place, but we must face reality. Forgive me for being blunt..."

She was even more worried by his statement. "What you say is true. Donald, my husband, and I had gone through medical school together. Without his support, I could never have made it on my own."

"You two are lucky; you have each other. How comforting it must be," he said, thinking about his own lack of support.

She smiled at his words. "I just wrote to tell him that I'm pregnant. He'll be shocked when he reads the letter."

23

"Dr. Colleen Mackey, congratulations. When I first saw you I knew that there was something special about you. You had that contented glow and air of peace that I envied so much. Now that you're expecting a baby, I understand your joy. Your husband is a lucky man."

Suddenly she was shocked at the level of intimacy of this conversation with a stranger. "I did not intend to burden you with my affairs, Chief. Please excuse me. Today has been a difficult one. I just lost a patient, an elderly lady that reminded me so much of my mother. I did all I could, but that was not enough." She was close to tears.

Nathan took her two hands in his. "Dr. Mackey, I'm glad you've spoken freely tonight. The world is in turmoil,, and our way of life is threatened by external events we can't control. I understand your anxiety, even your despair if that properly defines your emotions. A friend can sometimes make the load a little less burdensome. I would be honored to be your friend. In this time and place, we're two strangers, but two people can carry a load easier than one. This is only the second time I've met you, yet I don't feel like a stranger. If I'm being too bold, I apologize. I respect you very much, Dr. Mackey."

She turned away to put on her coat. "You're a kind man, Chief. You have not been too bold. I accept your offer of friendship. Thank you for sharing a moment of personal concern. Goodnight, I'll be back tomorrow. After that you should be fine. You're a quick healer, Chief."

"Goodnight, Dr. Mackey," he answered. The minute she left the room, he felt suddenly alone. His reaction disturbed him. Personal feelings had no place in his world. He made a vow to reign them in the next time they erupted.

Chapter Four

Coast Guard Station, Wells, Maine, Winter 1941-1942

Nathan's wound healed satisfactorily under the watchful care of Dr. Mackey. The station was adapting to the routines that had been established when operations began. Patrols were maintained daily, Sundays included. Those who wished to attend church services on Sunday were routed to postings that would allow them to do so. The Coast Guard encouraged regular church participation. On larger bases, those services were provided for the men. Nathan made available the Jeep and the truck for the eleven men who requested the opportunity.

Nathan had neglected the tradition that had been a fixed routine in his family for years. He thought it was time for him to re-establish a relationship with his Savior, Jesus Christ. He prayed frequently but never as intensely as when he was in combat and was afraid. It was a source of strength and comfort that he had turned to often.

One Sunday after Thanksgiving, Nathan, Jim and two of the seamen attended the Wells Baptist Church on Route One taking seats near the rear of the church.

When the minister opened services, he acknowledged their presence. "I see that we have some of our proud Coast Guardsmen with us this morning. Welcome to our small community church. We are proud to have you join us in praising the Lord. You are always in our prayers."

Nathan acknowledged the tribute with a smile and a nod of his head. He was glad that he came. All during the service he was thinking of a project he would discuss with the minister after services. The final hymn was his favorite, *Amazing Grace.*

Near the ending of the hymn the minister left the pulpit and made his way to the rear of the church, stopping at their pew.

"We would be honored if the four of you would accompany me to the entrance of the church where the congregation could say hello and shake your hands, gentlemen."

Nathan spoke for all of them. "We'd be glad to do that, Reverend." They were all dressed in their best uniforms. Nathan was a stickler for proper deportment. His Coasties looked especially sharp that morning.

They took their positions beside Reverend Pease as the parishioners began to leave the church. They were humbled by the sincerity and enthusiasm of the people to meet them. The younger men looked them over with interest while the young girls shyly smiled and said "hello" with admiring eyes. One of the elderly men told them that he had been a veteran of the U.S. Revenue Cutter Service prior to 1915.

One of the last to leave the church was Dr. Colleen Mackey. "You've recovered very well, Chief. It's nice to see you again."

"The privilege is mine, Doctor. It's nice to be appreciated by so many wonderful people."

"This is a very special town. I've felt welcome from day one." She shook hands with the other three men and left with an elderly lady walking towards her Ambassador.

After the last person departed from the church, Nathan turned to Reverend Pease. "I've been thinking, Reverend. What do you think about the Coast Guard hosting a Christmas party for families interested in visiting the station? We could show them what takes place in the tower and discuss our mission. It would be fun to share with the town what we are all about. I'm sure I could prod our master cook and baker to put on a meal for those who attend. An evening of fellowship and carol singing would be fun. We have a few good musicians in the company. What do you think?"

"I like your idea, Chief. I'm sure the parishioners would agree. We desperately need events to bring us closer together and to encourage mutual support for the dark days ahead. If you need a hand in organizing it, Chief, let me know. Give me your ideas on paper so that I can help spread the word."

"Thanks, Reverend. I'll be in touch." With that, Nathan shook his hand and rushed to the truck.

The area was blanketed with a light snow on Thanksgiving of 1941. Nathan had just inserted his last man at the Moody beach post and returned to the headquarters building with the relieved sentries. He joined the men in the dining room for a hot coffee and an apple turnover fresh out of the oven. While he was finishing his coffee, the baker told him that their shipment of milk and cream was ready at the Beach Farm on the road leading to Route One.

Nathan got back into the truck to pick up the milk at the farm, spending a few minutes with the owner, Mr. Ridley, discussing current events and the potential for the Wells detachment to be enlarged in the near future. On his way back, Nathan noticed an automobile off to the side of the road with a lone figure opening the trunk of the vehicle. He came to a stop behind the automobile, recognizing Dr. Mackey. Leaving the truck lights on and the engine running, he stepped out of the truck.

"Are you having trouble, Dr. Mackey?"

She was relieved to hear his voice. "Oh, yes. I have a flat tire. I was on my way to visit a family at the beach with the mumps."

"Do you have a spare?" he asked.

"I just checked. There's one in the trunk. The jack and wrench are with it."

"Now, may I ask a favor of you, Doctor?" He asked, recognizing that she was not dressed adequately for the cold and windy night air. "Please take a seat in the truck, and I'll change the tire for you."

She was shivering. "If you insist, but I can hold the light for you."

"If I need your help, I'll call you," he smiled and opened the door of the truck for her.

"I do feel chilled," she admitted. "Thank you, Chief Collins."

"I'm dressed for the cold. I'll have you back on the road in no time."

He placed the jack under the car and braced the front wheels with a block of wood he carried in the truck bed. Ten minutes later he had attached the good tire to the wheel and placed the flat one in the trunk of her Ambassador. He went to the driver side of the truck and asked for her keys, returning to her car to start the motor and turn the heater on full blast.

He returned to the truck and sat beside her. "Wait a few minutes for your Nash to warm up. Remember, you've got to take good care of yourself and that baby you're carrying," he smiled. "Now I'm sounding like the doctor."

"You're very kind, Chief. I really appreciate your help. I wasn't too sure if I could place the jack properly under the car. I'm glad you came by."

"So am I. Soldiers and Coasties always rescue damsels in distress. It's part of the job," he laughed heartily.

"I really should be going, Chief," she said, getting out of the warm truck.

"I understand," he said, opening the car door for her. "The people are lucky to have you in town, Dr. Mackey."

"Thanks for all of your support, Chief. Goodnight."

One week later, December 7, 1941, the world woke up to learn that which they had been dreading had finally taken place. The Japanese had attacked Pearl Harbor, a United States Naval Base in the Hawaiian Islands. The country was at war. Nathan had received early warnings that cancelled their attendance at church that Sunday. He informed the detachment what had taken place, having all of them stand by on an alert basis and to await additional orders. Several days passed. Due diligence was the order of the day. The Coast Guard had already been attached to the Navy two weeks prior to the Japanese attack. War was declared with Japan and, two days later, with Germany.

The nation faced the monumental task of fighting on two continents against two of the strongest and best trained military forces in history. A massive sense of urgency and anxiety gripped the nation. The outcome was uncertain. The United States had one of the smallest military forces in the world. Poor political decisions to limit the military of past decades were a cause for much regret. The armed forces of all the branches were now responsible for defending the nation with inadequate means available to do so.

The Coast Guard Detachment at Wells walked their posts with a new awareness of the potential danger that lurked across the dark waters of the Atlantic Ocean. Ships enroute to and from England off the New England coast were being destroyed by German submarines at an alarming rate. Almost nightly loud explosions on the horizon could be seen and heard. Fiery deaths took place within sight of the civilian population on the coast. Debris from the shipping wreckage washed ashore almost daily. Frequently dead bodies of sailors were amongst the flotsam. The Coasties watched the tides closer than ever, hoping that they might find a living survivor among the wreckage. Few survived the traumatic ordeal in the winter months. They were also alerted for German saboteurs attempting to come ashore. Nathan was told that intelligence estimates acknowledged the threat of German agents at any point along the Atlantic seaboard. They would be inserted ashore via submarine.

Two weeks after Pearl Harbor, Nathan received an urgent call from a sentry post that one of the men had broken a leg climbing among the slippery rocks. He left the tower to pick up the man and to replace him, ordering someone to call Dr. Mackey. An hour later, he carried the man into their infirmary room, carefully removing the man's coat and boots.

"That really hurts, Chief," cried the injured man, sitting up quickly in bed.

"Well, Nelson, I'll leave it until Dr. Mackey arrives. We could transport you to Portsmouth if you prefer."

"I trust Dr. Mackey, Chief. I'll go along with whatever she suggests," Nelson replied.

"Would you like a cup of coffee?"

"That would be great. It's cold out there. I apologize for being a bother, Chief. I should have been more careful."

"Nonsense, Nelson, accidents happen. If my nose is correct, I can smell an apple pie. What do you say if we sample a piece as soon as it comes from the oven?" Nathan grinned mischievously at the uncomfortable Nelson.

"I'm with you, Chief. The chow here is as good as I've ever had," Nelson replied.

While Nathan was getting coffee and checking on the pies, Dr. Mackey arrived, going directly to the infirmary room. She removed her coat and scarf, questioning Nelson, "I got here as quickly as I could. Which leg is injured?"

"It's my left one, Doctor. Chief Collins tried to remove my boot, but it hurt a lot," Nelson told her.

She gently felt his leg for bone splinters and cut the pant leg up to his thigh with a pair of scissors. The lower part of Nelson's leg was already black and blue and swollen. "I've got to remove your boot, young man. May I cut it off your foot?"

"Whatever you need to do, Dr. Mackey."

"I have a heavy pair of clippers for a situation such as this. I'll do it as carefully as possible, Seaman Nelson. Tell me if it hurts."

Nathan entered the room with coffee and apple pie. "I thought I heard you come in, Dr. Mackey. Nelson here had a bit of bad luck. Would you like some coffee?"

"Hello, Chief. I would like some coffee after we make Nelson a little more comfortable. As soon as I remove his boot I'll be able to determine if it's a bad sprain or a broken bone," she said, removing the last remnant of the boot. She dropped the clippers into her bag and examined Nelson's swollen ankle. It was black and blue up to his knee. She slowly felt the ankle with experienced fingers.

"Ouch," Nelson cried out.

"I think you're a lucky Coastie Nelson. I believe you have a bad sprain instead of a broken foot. You'll be laid up for a while, but we can make you comfortable."

"That's good news," Nathan remarked. "We can keep him here while he's recuperating instead of sending him to Portsmouth. It's up to you, Nelson."

"I prefer staying with my friends, Chief. That means someone will have to double up on my patrol post."

"Don't worry about that," Nathan assured him, watching the gentle doctor bath his foot in a brine solution before wrapping it tightly in large compression bandages.

Nelson had finished his coffee and pie by the time Dr. Mackey was finished. She gave him a mild sedative to help him sleep and to ease the pain. When she was finished, she turned to Nathan and said in a soft voice, "Now a cup of coffee would be welcome."

He motioned her to the dining room where the baker had set out two coffees and two pieces of warm apple pie. He could see that she was distressed. Dark circles and fine lines radiated beneath her eyes. She looked exhausted. He assumed that she was worrying about the situation that existed in the Philippines: the Japanese had invaded the islands with massive forces in several locations. He knew that her husband was stationed there and was concerned for her.

She represented thousands of other family members who were sitting glued to their radio sets for any information, good or bad, from China and the Orient or from Europe where the Germans were mercilessly capturing sovereign countries all over Europe. The German war machine was unleashed on their helpless neighbors while the brutal Japanese were rapidly occupying China, Korea, and islands in the Pacific towards Australia. The evening news programs tried to spread hope for the eventual outcome of the conflicts, but the seriousness of the reports did little to erase anxieties, even fear for the future. Those with loved ones serving in areas now being overrun were justifiably alarmed.

"I'm sure that you're concerned for your husband. When was the last time you heard from him? If you think my question is out of line, I apologize. I'm a friend who's concerned for a friend. Maybe it will help to talk about it."

She sighed and took a sip of her coffee. "I'm sick with worry, Chief. Everything exploded so quickly. I last heard from Donald on Thanksgiving Day. The Japanese have already captured some of the Philippine Islands. Why can't we stop their advance across the Pacific?" she asked angrily.

"You can blame the politicians for the lack of readiness of our armed forces. The surge of tyranny now taking place so quickly is bad but their greed for more territorial control may be a part of their undoing. Eventually, we'll be able to stop both the Germans and the Japanese. Take heart in the fact that

General MacArthur is in command of the forces now in the Philippines. He's one of our most able leaders," he said, trying to be more positive than he actually felt.

"I've been going on hope," she exclaimed in a soft voice. "Prayers have helped, but nothing can erase the horrible images that keep clouding my mind. I fear that it's going to be a long, bloody affair. I also know that I'm not alone in thinking as I do and feeling so helpless. I find some comfort in that fact."

"Now that we're officially in this war, I'm sure that I'll be rotated out of this command position and ordered to a cutter or to one of the destroyers the Navy is making available to the Coast Guard. My experience at sea will be needed. All of the services will be expanding rapidly. Any new recruit could handle this coastal security post," he told her, finishing his apple pie.

She was quiet for a moment and asked, "Is that what you want, Chief?"

He was quick to reply, "Oh, yes. I'm anxious to go back to sea. I'll miss this place. For the first time in my life I feel as if I belonged. The people have been special, and I'll always have a soft spot for them in my heart. You've contributed to my sense of well-being, Dr. Mackey. Your dedication and calm professionalism have been an inspiration to me. I'll miss your friendship."

"And you have been a source of strength for me and the community. Isn't it strange that the threat of war, and war itself, binds us in unions that make those unions stronger than the sum of the individuals...?"

He smiled at her. "I think I detect a philosopher beneath that physician's frock."

"Sometimes I get carried away with my thoughts." She returned his smile. "Thanks for the coffee and conversation. I'll be back tomorrow to see Nelson."

"I'll walk you to your automobile."

She put her coat on and picked up her black bag. He followed her outside and opened the car door for her. "Goodnight, Dr. Mackey. Until tomorrow."

"Thanks for everything, Chief Collins. We'll miss you if you're transferred. Until tomorrow."

As Christmas of 1941 approached, the country was completely engrossed in the execution of the war in Europe and in Asia. Men and women were joining the armed services by the thousands while those in industry converted their manufacturing facilities for the production of war goods. The arsenal of democracy was rolling up its collective shirtsleeves to defeat the common foes. Despair and anxiety resided in every home, yet, there was a determined effort for everyone to do their share. There were few shirkers, and they were quickly shunned. Sharing of sacrifices drew the country together physically and emotionally. The war demanded and received unanimous effort.

It was in the spirit of joining together in common cause that prompted Reverend Pease and Chief Collins and his detachment to sponsor a Christmas party for children and adults. It was set up to last for a couple of hours between four and six in the afternoon at the Coast Guard dining room. It had been supplemented with additional chairs and tables from the church's hall. The Coasties had decorated the dining room and a large balsam fir Christmas tree with a star at the very top.

Without a doubt the biggest attraction for young and old alike had been the cement observation tower. Coasties accompanied groups of ten each up the stairs to the observation platform where they were shown the powerful telescopes used to detect movement on a wide-angle view far out on the horizon. Each child and adult was given a chance to look through the scope. They were excited to see a large freighter heading on a northern track. The numbers on the superstructure could be seen easily. The ship was probably on its way to Halifax, Nova Scotia, where the transports were formed into massive convoys for the crossing to the British Isles or to Murmansk, Russia.

A fifty-caliber machine gun was positioned just below the observation platform. A short burst of a few rounds demonstrated that the Coasties were prepared to defend themselves if necessary. Most left the tower with a sober expression and returned to the festivities at the dining room.

A piano had been pulled out of the large barn and tuned for the occasion. Will Goode was a young Coastie with red hair and freckles around his nose. He was a good piano player and played several short medleys of Christmas carols and popular favorites while the group sat in fellowship eating a meal prepared by the Coast Guard cooks. When all were seated and served, Rev. Pease rose and held out his hands for silence.

"We are gathered together here in this Coast Guard facility to celebrate the birthday of Jesus Christ. Our hosts have been most generous and gracious, and we thank them for their hospitality. They are representative of all the men and women who are sacrificing much for our country so that we can live in peace and freedom. We pray that God will watch over them and keep them safe from harm. We ask it in Christ's name, Amen."

Jim Reams had helped with the serving of the guests and took a seat next to Rev. Pease and Dr. Mackey. The Reverend patted him on the shoulder: "This has been a pleasant respite, especially for the children. I think it has given them a better appreciation for the efforts being made for our protection."

"Thanks, Reverend. The Chief has this detachment running like a fine watch," Jim replied.

Suddenly they heard bells ringing outside and a loud voice hollering out for Dasher and Dancer to stop..."

Jim stood up and announced, "I hear Santa Claus!"

Santa burst through the door with a flourish and a loud "Merry Christmas, ho, ho, ho..." Dressed in a red suit with white fur trimmings and a massive white beard, he rushed to the far end of the dining room with a large white sack over his shoulder. The kids were excited.

"I'm on my way from the North Pole to see if you boys and girls have been good. This is a very special day for me, ho, ho, ho."

Santa went to each individual, children and adults, with a colorfully wrapped gift for each, asking them if they have been good. It was obvious that Santa was enjoying himself. Seaman Goode was softly playing *Jingle Bells* when Santa came up to him patting his red hair. "I tried to enlist this boy as one of my elves, but he was too tall to ride in my sleigh, ho, ho, ho."

Continuing down the line Santa gave each a gift made up of chocolate, peanuts and gum. Much of it came from their military C-rations. When he came before Reverend Pease, who was slightly overweight, Santa placed a gift in front of him. "Have you been good, Rev?"

The good Reverend acknowledged that he had tried. "Ho, ho, ho," Santa hollered in a loud voice, pounding on his large belly. "Go easy on the chocolate, Rev, or you'll look like me." No one laughed harder than the Reverend Pease.

Then Santa side-stepped in front of Jim, "I have it on good authority that you've been good, except that you've been bribing the baker for additional apple pies. Be careful, boy, or you'll be like me, ho, ho, ho," Santa said with a flourish, slapping his belly again.

"Last but not least, we come to our remarkable Dr. Mackey who blossoms with goodness," Santa announced, looking in his sack. "Somewhere in this sack is a very special gift..." He placed the sack on the table and spent several seconds rummaging through it. "Ah, finally. We saved the best for the last," he announced in his booming voice, leaving a small gift in front of Dr. Mackey. "Merry Christmas to all and to all a goodnight."

Santa then stomped out the door. A few minutes later, they heard the tinkle of bells and his booming voice: "Ho, ho, ho, away we go."

It was a night enjoyed by all, ending on a happy note. Shortly after the guests departed the dining hall. Jim and Rev. Pease congratulated every guest as they walked out the door. Dr. Mackey remained at her seat. When she was alone, she opened the gift. It was a small velvet box containing a crucifix with palm leaves wrapped around the cross with the words "Hope is Eternal" etched on the cross. She clasped it tightly and quietly left the dining room with moist eyes.

Chapter Five

Coast Guard Station Wells, Maine, Winter 1942

The winter of 1942 was long and severe. The nation was at war. The people did not realize it then, but it was our nation's finest hour. From the shore of the Pacific to the forestlands of Maine, the people rallied to subdue the common enemy. A feeling of purpose and unity and dedication permeated the land, accompanied by a profound sadness to those who bore the losses of loved ones in the cause of liberty.

One cold evening in January while a northeaster was snowing and blowing, and visibility was limited, the sentry post closest to the observation tower sent an anxious call for assistance. The sentry had not seen anything, but heard a distinct muffled sound of a person coughing. He requested lights and backup. The Maine State Police barracks in Wells was available for emergencies. They could also isolate the coastline from access to Route One by blocking the road leading to Moody while the Coast Guard blocked access along the coastline. If German agents tried to penetrate their security, they would pick conditions that existed that evening.

Nathan was at the tower when the call came in and led a relief squad to the location in the Jeep which had a powerful search light attached to a mount beside the machine gun. The sentry on duty directed them inland once they had secured the beachhead for evidence of a landing. The team saw no tracks or marks in the sand.

Either the sentry was wrong, or the suspects had already cleared the beach. That left the pitch pine wooded area and the marsh immediately across the road. Nathan looked up and down the roadway for prints in the recent snow. They found several that had crossed the road into the stand of trees. The Coasties grabbed their flashlights and took to the area with pistols drawn. Nathan had them fan out about twenty feet apart.

They found two men hiding behind a log and ordered them to step into the light and identify themselves. They answered with a volley of gunfire that hit Nathan in his leg, spinning him around, knocking him to the ground. The men instantly responded with return fire and charged the defensive position. One of the men had been hit and was lying on the ground bleeding on the white snow. The second man surrendered without resistance. The Maine State Police arrived at that moment offering to take custody of the men. Everyone's attention then turned to Nathan and the wounded prisoner.

Nathan had dropped his flashlight in the snow when the bullet knocked his leg out from under him. He quickly retrieved the light and examined his leg. The bullet had penetrated the calf of his left leg. It was bleeding heavily. Will Goode began to bandage his leg to stop the bleeding.

"Can you move your leg, Chief?" Will asked.

"I'm not sure," Nathan replied. "Help me up." One of the troopers leaped to assist Will just as Nathan passed out.

Later, Nathan remembered being carried to the Jeep where he was held in a seat during a wild ride to the station. The men carried him into the infirmary room. The cook and baker cut away his trousers so that they could determine how badly he was injured. He was still bleeding heavily and had lost a lot of blood. He felt dizzy and disoriented.

"Can you hear me, Chief?" Jim had asked, wrapping a blanket around him.

"Tell me what happened, Jim," Nathan asked, closing his eyes and resting against the pillow.

"Well, Chief, the State Police have stopped a car traveling down towards the beach from Route One. It turned out to be the pickup vehicle for the two men. One was wounded resisting arrest. Both are in custody of the State Police. You took a direct hit in the leg from one of the German agents who were well armed. We've called Dr. Mackey for you. Rest easy, Chief.

You've lost a lot of blood. Could you drink a cup of coffee or some ginger ale? You need to take some liquids."

"Coffee would be great, Jim. Would you please crank me up so that I can see better? We were lucky tonight. Goode's instincts were correct. I guess an ear for music helps on sentry duty. Tell him thanks for me, Jim."

"I already have, Chief. He's still at his post."

Dr. Mackey entered the room breathing heavily. She had rushed as quickly as possible when she received word that a man had been shot. When she saw that the man was Nathan, she scolded him playfully. "Chief, you have a knack of being at the wrong place at the wrong time." She threw her coat on a nearby chair and anxiously checked his leg. "Are you in pain, Chief?"

"Not as much as I thought it would hurt," he replied. "Is the bone broken?"

She carefully examined the leg with her trained hands. "I don't think it's broken, but the bullet is still in you and has to come out. I'll have to probe for it, Chief. It may hurt. I can give you a powerful pain killer. The choice is yours."

"Do what you have to do, Dr. Mackey. I don't like a lot of medicine."

"I'll go slowly with the probe," she explained, dipping it in alcohol. "We've got to locate the bullet first."

She grabbed the calf of his leg and squeezed it hard. He flinched when she located the lead slug. It was pressed against a nerve. She removed the probe and selected a slender pair of forceps, knowing that the next move was going to be painful. She inserted the forceps deep into the wound and deftly grabbed the lead, pulling it from the bleeding wound, dropping it in a saucer on the table beside his bed. All the time he had been grinding his teeth, determined to not cry out. Surprisingly the pain subsided as soon as she removed the bullet.

He reached for it and examined it closely. "It's a 9mm from a German Luger pistol. It felt as if a truck had hit me."

"You were lucky, Chief," she soberly told him, cleaning the wound with antiseptics. "I'll dress it with a tight compress bandage. You'll continue to bleed some. By tomorrow it should be clotting. I'll redo the dressing then. You should rest easy for the next few days to give the wound a chance to heal properly."

He grinned at her. "You know this is probably going to get me transferred. I understand that the regional headquarters have a few newly commissioned ensigns on standby as replacements. If that happens, I'll miss this duty station."

"We'll all miss you, Chief. Your performance as Santa Claus will be a hard one to follow," she said, covering him with another blanket. "Santa's gift has touched me, and I'm grateful for friends who care. Thank you."

"You're welcome, Dr. Mackey. It was nice of you to respond again for help. I promise to rest as you suggest. It was worth getting hit. We stopped two German agents from carrying out their dirty deeds. I'm thankful for that."

"I've got to go, Chief. I'll see you tomorrow afternoon. I'm relieved. When I got the call about a gunshot wound I expected it to be more severe. This horrible war has already caused enough heartache, and it looks as if it's going to be a long and difficult time. I'm already exhausted…"

Nathan grasped her hand. "Be brave, dear lady. We're being tested now, but we'll survive this war. Do not be discouraged. We need people like you to help hold the home front together. You're a symbol of what this war is all about. Soon you'll be a mother, too. I join you in praying for your husband. Do not lose hope, Dr. Mackey. Thanks for taking care of me."

"Goodnight, Chief."

That evening Nathan received notice of his transfer to the Portsmouth Navy Yard Hospital. A young Coast Guard ensign would report the next day to assume duties as commanding officer of the Wells detachment. The communiqué congratulated him and the detachment with a "well done." Praise from the area commander always made the men feel appreciated.

The next morning, Nathan was surprised to receive a visit from his mother and little Casey who was walking and starting to talk quite a bit. He placed his head on the pillow next to his father's head and curiously looked into his eyes. "I love you, Daddy."

The words touched a part of Nathan that he had been denying for a long time. His son represented the betrayal of his wife. As long as he was busy with his mind occupied on other matters, he was able to cope with that loss. Now he had to confront it again. He knew that denial could serve him for a limited time. Surprisingly he was overjoyed holding his son next to him on the bed.

He visited with his mother and discussed events back home in Belfast for several minutes when she confronted him with a serious expression on her face. "Son, I've got something to tell you… I've been trying to come up with the right words."

"What's wrong, Ma? Is Pa okay?"

"Yes, your father is fine. I, I have to tell you that Shirley is outside in the car. She returned a month ago and begged us for forgiveness. To make a long story short, she found that she had made a terrible mistake and wanted to return to Belfast to care for Casey. I must say that she has proven to be a good mother to your son."

"What are you trying to say, Ma?" cried Nathan, sitting up in bed.

"Do you want to see her? She said she would not come in unless you specifically asked for her."

"Do you know what she did to me, Ma? Am I supposed to just forget the brush-off she handed to Casey and me? I've hated her for doing that to us. It made me feel cheap like an old pair of shoes you throw away when finished with them." Nathan had worked himself into an angry state of mind.

His mother sighed, understanding his anger. "I don't blame you for feeling that way, son. I promised to make the trip with her. She said it was probably a wasted trip, but I was willing to go along in case you might change your mind. It was worth a try, son. The decision is yours."

"Where's her lover-boy friend?" Nathan asked in a sarcastic tone. "No, I don't want to see her right now, Ma."

Mrs. Collins rose from her chair. "We'll be leaving now. Don't be angry with us, son. We wanted you to see Casey, and we were worried about your being wounded. Chief Reams called us last night."

"I'm not angry at you, Ma. It has been nice seeing Casey and you. He's growing like a weed, isn't he? I love you very much, Ma. Don't be disappointed with my refusal."

"I really do understand your position, son. Get well soon. Good-bye."

"Good-bye, Ma, and to you too little man," Nathan hugged them both and watched them walk out the door with blurred vision. A part of him wanted to scream to them that he had changed his mind. How he yearned to hold Shirley the way he had before she left him. He had searched his performance and never came up with a good reason for her betrayal. Possibly it could have been his absence for long periods at a time, but that should have only strengthened the bond of love, especially with little Casey's addition to their lives.

Ensign Andrews reported for duty with Commander Schultz accompanying him the morning after his mother's visit. They went directly to the infirmary room, finding Nathan sitting up in bed drinking coffee.

"Good morning, Chief. I was concerned about you. You and your detachment have done a fine job and we're proud of your performance. This is Ensign Andrews, your relief officer. How are you feeling, Chief?"

"I apologize how I must look, Sir. The Wells detachment is a fine bunch of men, Ensign Andrews. It was a privilege to command them. I wish you luck. To be honest, Commander, this wound is not going to interfere with my duties here. My relief is a little sudden."

"I'm glad to meet you, Chief Collins," Ensign Andrews, a tall thin young man with that confident air so typical of recent graduates from the United States Coast Guard Academy at Newport, Connecticut. "It looks as if the Germans picked the wrong place to insert enemy agents into the country."

"We were lucky, Sir."

"I've got a number of stops to make, so I'll be on my way," Commander Schultz told them. "Ensign Andrews has orders to take over your command today. You're going to Portsmouth until you're fit to leave the hospital. I've given you a week's furlough, after which you'll report to my headquarters for duty in the North Atlantic, Chief. By the way, it looks as if the local

41

doctor is doing a fine job. I like it when we can utilize local services. It brings us closer to the people we serve."

"You certainly made a wise choice with Dr. Mackey, Sir," Nathan replied with a smile. "A few days at home will be welcome."

Jim Reams returned from the sentry posts and took Ensign Andrews on a tour of his new responsibility. While they were gone, Dr. Mackey arrived to check on Nathan's leg. He told her about the orders. "As soon as you're finished with me, I'll be transported to Portsmouth."

"I'm sure the men will miss you, Chief," she said, taking his pulse and temperature, thrusting a thermometer into his mouth. "Does the wound hurt?"

He replied after she removed the thermometer. "No."

She was beginning to show her pregnancy. Her mild disposition was always an important part of her make-up. The child she was carrying was a source of much joy, measurable by those who knew her well. Nathan had picked up on that part of her. Modest, professional and comfortable with who and what she was, Colleen was a woman at peace with herself. She carried her concern and worries deep within her heart, but at times he saw the sad eyes and that distant stare in moments of reflection.

They met as total strangers; now, when he was about to leave the area, she had become more than a comforting physician — they had become friends. She removed his old dressing and replaced it with a fresh one, nodding her approval with the way it was beginning to heal.

"Your wound looks good, Chief. Have you tried to stand up?"

"Not yet," he laughed. "I've been lazy, Doc. This infirmary bed is more comfortable than my old Army cot."

"Well, let's see how you feel putting some weight on the leg. I'll help you," she suggested, placing his slippers so that he could put them on.

He sat up on the edge, slipping his feet into the slippers. He placed his right arm around her for support and slowly stood up. She steadied him. Suddenly, Nathan looked down into her brown eyes and kissed her. She returned the kiss and immediately turned away.

He sat down on the bed, crushed by his precipitant action. "Forgive me. I'm out of bounds. I had no right to do that," he cried.

She turned to confront him with tears welling into her eyes, and said in a soft voice, "Chief Collins, what just happened was beautiful and spontaneous. Perhaps, at some other time and place things could be different, but for now, it's dangerous and reckless to encourage feelings we believe are present. You'll always have a special place in my heart as a friend. Beyond that, we must not entertain."

Chapter Six

Nathan wistfully looked up at the abandoned Coast Guard observation tower, remembering how it had been when the war first started in 1941. His faithful and efficient assistant, Jim Reams, was killed in action in the North Atlantic and was buried in the dark, cold waters. The costly convoys that ran from the United States and Nova Scotia to England and to the northern port of Murmansk, Russia, had taken the lives of thousands of seamen and destroyed hundreds of ships of all descriptions. The war at sea had been a deadly endeavor that was won solely by the fortitude of the brave merchant seamen manning the lumbering freighters and the high spirited escorts that valiantly tried to defend their passage through the dangerous waters.

The old cement tower had changed hands several times since the war ended. One owner had converted it to a restaurant and built an addition to seat more customers. Now it was badly in need of paint and repairs, and the open field that ran down to the water's edge was overgrown with small saplings and brush. The private home that had served as barracks and as headquarters was well maintained and beautifully landscaped, with a large fence around the property.

Nathan sighed and stood up to stretch his legs. Eighteen years had passed since he left Wells. That was a bench-mark year for him. Everything in his life was referenced to that time and to this place. How well he remembered! At every turn in his life since those dark days of the war he always came back to Wells. Sometimes physically and often emotionally. Here he had known contentment and had found peace of mind even though the most destructive war in history was raging all over the world.

He never deceived himself. His memories of the few moments he had spent with Dr. Colleen Mackey were locked in his consciousness. There was something illusively attractive about her he could never rationalize or explain. He was saddened when he left Wells that winter of 1942. She was married and carried another's man child! It was madness, and he could not help himself. The words she had softly spoken to him at their parting still echoed through his mind — "…perhaps, at some other time and place, things could be different… Beyond that we must not entertain."

Did she feel the same magnetism? He never knew for sure. To allow additional fantasies to grow to fruition could be dangerous to his mental well-being. He had yearned for what could never be! He had accepted that reality and was fully aware of the dangers, yet that attraction for a country doctor that he barely knew never left him. Over the years, he had become a more reflective person. His experience at Wells had been a stepping stone in his journey through life. Now, in the mature years of his life, the desire to turn back the years was just as strong as ever, perhaps even more so because the grains of sand in his own personal time capsule were slowly running out.

The most traumatic period of his Coast Guard career took place after he left Wells. Jim Reams had transported him to the Portsmouth Navy Yard Hospital. Two days later, he was on his way to Belfast, Maine, for a week-long furlough on a Boston and Maine bus. His wound was healing satisfactorily. Commander Schultz had told him that when he returned to duty it would be on a brand new Coast Guard cutter that was undergoing sea trials at that time.

The furlough home that winter had given him a chance to get better acquainted with his son, Casey. He had arrived at the bus station in town and called for his father to come get him. They lived about eight miles out in the country in a small bungalow surrounded with about two hundred acres of woodland. His father worked as a machinist on the small ferries that serviced the numerous islands off the coast of Maine.

His father picked him up in their 1933 Chevrolet sedan. It was a dependable vehicle that became a member of the family. He and his sister, Aline, had learned to drive it and took tests for their licenses with the vehicle. It had a clutch that chattered slightly when it was released, causing the car to jump forward. The family got used to the car's idiosyncrasies. Occasionally it needed a front end alignment when it began to shimmy.

His father leaped from the Chevy and embraced Nathan. "You look good to me, son. It's nice to have you home for a few days. We're awfully proud of the fact that you helped capture a German espionage agent."

Nathan placed an arm around his father and walked to the car. His father was a small, wiry man with expressive eyes. They were good friends and spent a lot of time together going fishing and hunting in the forest they both loved. Nathan found a parallel with the vast forests of Maine and the open ocean waters that connected continents. They both gave him a sense of well-being. The tranquility and solitude he always searched for was never lacking in either environment.

"We were lucky, Pa. I had some good men with me. How is Casey doing with Shirley?"

His father knew that it was a touchy subject. "They're doing okay, son. We see them often. As a matter of fact, she brought him over to our house when she heard that you were coming home for a few days so that you could spend some time with him."

Nathan shook his head. "I don't understand that woman. What does she think? Am I to simply forget what she did right out of the blue without warning? She put me through hell, and I haven't been able to understand what went wrong."

"She's a good mother to Casey, and she has asked us for forgiveness, son," his father explained. "I can't ever know what is in your heart or the depth of pain you experienced, especially with you at sea in the Coast Guard. Your mother and I understand what an awkward situation now exists between the two of you, and you'll have to settle it. Whichever way you decide, son, we support you. As long as Shirley continues to be responsible, we'll enjoy being grandparents to Casey. He deserves that, Nathan."

"I agree, Pa."

Nathan watched the familiar places where he had grown up. He dearly loved the town and the people in it. Their home was a few miles inland from the coast where they always accumulated more snow than their friends right on the waterfront. The winters in Maine were always severe. They had conditioned him so that duty in the North Atlantic did not alarm him as much as men from other parts of the country.

That furlough remained vivid in his memory. The day after his arrival, Nathan took Casey back to his mother at the small apartment she had rented. It was a four-room apartment on the second floor at the rear of a large Victorian home, fronting the ocean. The flesh wound on his leg was healing satisfactorily, allowing him to move about without pain. Shirley had not seen him in his new chief petty officer's uniform, which was very similar to that of a commissioned officer.

He rang the buzzer holding two-year-old Casey's hand. Shirley opened the door, her face filled with anxiety and uncertainty. "Come in, Nathan. Hi, Casey. Did you have fun with your daddy?"

The apartment was neat and clean as he remembered it. She had always been a good housekeeper like his mother. He was nervous stepping back into the familiar apartment. The subtle scent of heliotrope filled his senses. He recalled that she had always kept several plants in the kitchen. The scent brought back fond memories that had quickly turned to angry reflections.

"Shirley, we've got to talk," he had cried out, filled with emotions he did not understand.

"Let me take Casey's winter clothes off so that he can play in his room. Yes," she replied in a wavering voice, avoiding eye contact. "We do have to talk…"

He unbuttoned his great coat placing it on a peg in the hallway entrance. She took Casey into his room. Two minutes later she returned with moist eyes. "I know that what I did to you and to Casey is a gross injustice, and I have no right to ask for your forgiveness. You are blameless in the cheap and sordid act. You have every right to ask why, but I can't give any logical answer to why I was swayed by a smooth, slick line that swept me off my feet."

They sat at the small table in the kitchen. Nathan listened to her every word. "The girl who abandoned a marriage and a son so easily was not the same girl I went to school with and fell in love with. Was I so blind?" he asked bluntly.

"My folks, especially my sister Lena, have been outraged with my actions. I have betrayed everyone I ever loved and respected. I admit to that betrayal, but in the same breath, I beg your forgiveness. Hurting you was cruel. I have no excuses except that it happened…"

"You ask for forgiveness which comes easy to a person in love. How does one forget that it happened and may wonder if it is going to happen again in the future?" he soberly and forcefully questioned.

Shirley wiped the tears from her eyes, thankful that it had not turned into a shouting match. "I broke a sacred vow, and in the process, I like to think that I've grown. I'm ashamed of myself, and I beg you for another chance, Nat. Can we strike a truce? I want to be worthy of your love again. I'm willing to try if you agree. I'm frightened about what I've done to our relationship and with you returning to duty with the war raging just off our coast."

He quietly listened to her proposal all the time witnessing the agony she was going through. She was running on nerves. An air of doubt and desperation filled the small kitchen. She had begged for another chance. Was he capable of granting it to her? He was still uncertain, but he thought that the compromise was worthy of speculation.

"What do we have to lose?" he asked. "Casey deserves that from us."

"Oh, Nat," she cried, leaping into his arms. "Hold me, Nat. Hold me …"

He was powerless to refuse…

That reunion had sustained him as he prepared for the most traumatic assignment of his career in the Coast Guard. His first posting was on a brand new two hundred seventy-foot cutter, *Northland,* with a range of ten thousand miles before refueling. It was manned by fourteen officers and eighty-six enlisted men. Its top speed was about twenty knots loaded down with several tons of new equipment and armament. That was slower than some submarines, but it was superior in maneuverability and its ability to withstand high seas. They rolled and twisted in heavy seas much like a bucking Texas bronco, but they were a deadly combatant to the German submarines.

Sea trials had already been performed when Nathan was assigned to the cutter in Portsmouth, Virginia. He became responsible for the installation of new depth charges that were hurled into the air in a square configuration from several metal tubes much like a mortar. They were fired to blanket an area in conjunction with destroyers and other escort ships when available. This new depth charge could cover a larger area than the older ashcan type that were rolled off the stern of a ship.

The newly equipped cutter sailed out of Portsmouth fully armed with depth charges; twenty mm Bofor antiaircraft guns; ten fifty caliber machine gun mounts; and the forward three inch automatic cannon. The ship and the men were looking for trouble and they would run into more than they bargained for, testing themselves and their craft to the limit in the boiling seas of the North Atlantic where the Germans had infected the area with countless submarines. Their silent approach and attack tested the nerves of every sailor who ever served in the harsh waters that included the frozen Arctic. Out of the darkness of the arctic winter, death and destruction hit without warning, smashing heavily loaded freighters into smaller pieces that soon settled out of sight as if they had never been present.

Nathan's maiden voyage on the *Northland* was still locked into his consciousness. They had left Portsmouth with two Navy destroyers for Halifax, Nova Scotia. Twenty heavily loaded freighters were patiently waiting for their escorts. They were the life-line that kept England, an island nation, in the war. They crossed the Atlantic south of Greenland and Iceland, arriving at the western approaches to the dangerous waters around the British Isles. That first convoy lost two ships to submarine attack only a short distance from port. German planes from France and Norway attacked the convoy on a daily basis, weather permitting.

The first ship to be torpedoed was at night. Two direct hits severed the ship's superstructure into three parts. The center portion exploded, sending debris and men into the air. Nathan recalled seeing a man thrown into the air where he paused for several seconds before dropping into the fiery cauldron. The sight made him nauseous, and he leaned over the rail to empty his stomach.

The loss of two ships was bad enough, but the one that followed in their wake lost twenty-four ships out of thirty-nine. The butchery was unbelievable. The *Northland* had started its return voyage when it was ordered to assist the following convoy in any way possible. They responded at top speed. The convoy was ordered to scatter and to continue in a zig-zag pattern of travel to minimize losses.

They trolled the dark waters searching for survivors. The debris field was covered several inches thick with crude oil. Few individuals survived the oil-covered icy waters. Twelve terrorized men with deep-set eyes were pulled from the jaws of death. It was these kinds of retrieval operations that distinguished the seamanship and expertise of the Coast Guard. Life-saving was their primary mission, and they were proud that they had molded the crew of the *Northland* into a professional force with few equals. Their rapid response and successful implementation of snatching floundering men from certain death was appreciated by every seaman who witnessed their performance. At any given time the Coasties knew that they could be a target for the lurking U-boats. That fact never lessened their life-saving efforts.

The North Atlantic and the frozen Arctic cultivated and nurtured deep-seated anxieties in every man's heart that sailed the northern approaches in the dead of winter. Yet Nathan developed a fascination for their lonely vigil in the vast unfriendly northern latitudes. The area triggered a dark mood that made man reflect on his own mortality. Self-sufficiency was a given virtue, yet there was an even more powerful dependence placed on companions who shared the same feelings and the same anxiety about the environment. They were a safety net for the inevitable curse of fate that constantly tested one's mettle in life and death situations. Friendships became more meaningful and, at times, the last resource to survival in the north. An unspoken brotherhood unites men in the northern latitudes more than in any other hemisphere.

The Coast Guard was given the mission of establishing and supplying several weather stations along the eastern coastline of Greenland, a part of Denmark which was occupied by German troops in the spring of 1940. Aside from acting as an escort for convoys along the route, they established navigational aids and alerted authorities of severe weather conditions. The Coast Guard also conducted search and rescue operations for downed pilots and shipwrecked sailors within their sphere of operations.

Accurate weather predicting in Europe depended on precise weather conditions prevailing in the frozen northern latitudes. Therefore, weather stations became as important to the Germans as to the Allies in conducting any type of operations involving aircraft or naval ships. Weather predictions were a vital part of every military response to the Germans. Denmark had several permanent stations along the eastern coast of Iceland and the southern half of the east coast of Greenland. The northern half of the country was a frozen wasteland.

The *Northland* escorted one convoy up to the northern approaches where the Royal Navy took over responsibility for the safety of the convoy. The Coast Guard cutter was given new orders to proceed to the Denmark Straits northwest of Iceland after they had been loaded to capacity with food and other supplies to conduct a reconnaissance of the eastern coast of Greenland. Intelligence indicated that scattered among the numerous bays and inlets were several German weather stations. Their orders were to capture the men and equipment if at all possible, or to destroy them if they resisted. It was the kind of mission that the professional crew was fully capable of executing.

When they stopped at Reykjavik, Iceland, for added supplies, Nathan made sure that they obtained adequate firearms and ammunition for the proposed landing parties which were his responsibility. A large Army freighter was in the harbor supplying the Army detachment that was relieving the marines previously stationed in Iceland. The Army supplied the Coast Guard with twenty-five new semi-automatic Garand rifles, a dozen Thompson sub-machine guns, and a supply of hand grenades. Part of their equipment was three radio transmitters and two hand cranked generators all suitable for use in arctic weather. The storage compartments of the cutter were jammed full of precious supplies and equipment.

The day they left Reykjavik Nathan was called into the Captain's quarters. Lieutenant Joel Andrews was an experienced officer who ran a tight ship. He demanded and received the best the men were capable of giving. His unassuming disposition endeared him to the men. He rarely shouted orders. Instead he suggested that this or that should be done, and it was generally taken care of. Breaches of discipline could be severe, and no one ever questioned who was in command.

Nathan liked the captain and announced his presence as he entered the small quarters. "Did you wish to see me, Captain?"

Captain Andrews was sitting at his desk covered with papers. "Come in, Chief. Please, take a seat. I want to talk with you about an unusual request."

Nathan noticed a large navigational chart of the rugged east coast of Greenland on the Captain's desk. "I've stored some of the landing party's supplies in the engine room where they'll be a little drier."

Captain nodded his approval and pointed to the map on his desk. "I've just received a priority communication from Atlantic Naval Command. They want us to form a four-man patrol for the express purpose of searching Greenland's eastern coast for German radio weather reporting stations. Two or three Eskimo sled drivers will accompany the patrol. The intent is to proceed as far north as is humanly possible."

Nathan listened carefully to the captain's description of an operation beyond his experience capabilities. "Do we have the right equipment for such an operation, Sir? That's uncharted frozen wasteland!"

"I called you in here to ask if you would head up such a patrol. I will not order you to accept it, Chief. If you tell me 'no' that will be the end of it, and I'll tell Atlantic Command that the Army will have to do it."

"Can I pick my men, Sir?"

"Of course, Chief."

"Okay, then, I'm your man. I may be crazy, but there's a part of the arctic that fascinates me."

"We're due for refueling with a Navy tanker," Captain Andrews told him. "I hope to pick up our mail and a supply of current reading material to help you pass the time on your northern trek, Chief. I've spent some time in Iceland and on Shannon Island, Greenland. I know from experience that basic attention to caring for oneself in the Arctic is most important. Its isolation and eerie quiet can get to a person who is not prepared for its challenges. Some men are driven mad by its ominous threat to life, yet I found it renewing and beautiful. I have a feeling that you will respond to it with similar emotions, Chief."

Nathan carefully listened to his captain, hoping that his words would be prophetic. A few hours after their conversation they were being refueled by the tanker. Everyone on the ship received several week's accumulation of mail. Nathan had a few letters from Shirley and his parents. He was surprised that he did not have more from his wife. The last one was dated October 12, 1942. It was a long letter full of gossip about friends and homey descriptions of Casey's activities. There was an air of detachment about the letter that alarmed him. Picking up a letter from his mother, anxious for any word from home, Nathan received news that struck him like a physical blow. He read the letter a second time hoping that he had missed something:

Dear Son,

Tonight, we are saddened to inform you that Shirley has died at the local hospital. After you returned to duty, she found out that she was pregnant from her boy-friend. Frightened about the potential of destroying your marriage, she found a person who agreed to abort the child. To make a long story short, she bled to death from the abortion even though she was rushed to the hospital... it was too late. She died shortly after...

I'm so sorry,

Love Mom and Dad

Chapter Seven

North Atlantic – 1942-1943

The early fall and winter of 1942 was the most traumatic period of Nathan's life. The sudden death of Shirley, the mother of his son, under the conditions described in his mother's last letter almost drove him to the brink of madness. His inability to understand the chaotic circumstances surrounding her decision to seek an abortion from a medical quack in the back room of his office fueled a desire to lash out in protest to the injustice heaped upon him.

He had just committed himself to the most dangerous mission of his career. Now he was obsessed about being so far from home when such a bizarre incident turned his world inside out. For days he carried out his duties on the cutter in an advanced state of mental fatigue. His conduct was not ignored by Captain Andrews who asked for permission to enter the chief's wardroom where Nathan was sipping a cup of coffee. "May I join you, Chief?"

Nathan instinctively knew that his erratic behavior warranted a talk from the captain. "Please do, Sir," he replied.

"Chief, you've got me worried. The Army is pressing me for a decision about the subject we discussed earlier. I had notified Army command that we had a man competent enough to conduct such a long, arduous patrol in uncharted territory. Since then, I've observed a different man. I'm sure that your reasons are personal, and I certainly do not want to get involved in my men's private affairs. However, I've got to have a definitive answer for the Army. If you feel that you cannot do the mission, tell me now. Either you or the Army will take the job. Whoever takes it, the *Northland* will steam along the eastern coast of Greenland prepared to insert a team and their supplies. Unless you assure me that you can handle the mission, I will cancel out. Your recent behavior has not been up to your normal standard. Do you have anything to say, Chief?"

Nathan understood his captain's predicament. Holding back nothing, Nathan confided to him what had taken place back home. To his amazement, the minute he finished, Nathan felt relieved. The chance to just talk about his problem helped him to accept the tragedy for what it was. The way he had described the situation to Captain Andrews gave him another perspective on Shirley's desire to rid her body of another man's seed. It was a tribute to the love they had shared. Her desire to keep the hurtful information from him was interpreted by him as an act of love. That concept brought tears to his eyes, and he buried his head on his folded arms on the mess table weeping uncontrollably.

Captain Andrews witnessed the catharsis and placed a comforting hand on Nathan's trembling shoulder. At that moment, another chief entered the wardroom seeking a cup of coffee. He noticed Nathan and quietly left the room. Several minutes later, Nathan lifted his head to wipe his eyes with his shirtsleeve. "I apologize for my outburst, Sir."

"Every man has his breaking point, Chief. You simply proved that you're a human being. The tragedy you've experienced is enough to burden any person, especially being so far away from the problem at a time of war. I'll leave you to make up your mind about the Greenland patrol. I'll support whatever you decide."

Captain Andrews turned to leave. Nathan stood with him and said, "If you think I'm still capable of handling the patrol, then I'd like to carry out the mission."

"As far as I'm concerned that settles it, Chief. I'll contact our Army brothers and set up a rendezvous for our Coast Guard team and the native Eskimos with the dog teams. I'm proud to recommend you. I suggest that you assemble your team and double-check your equipment. If you have mail to be sent out, I'll personally dispatch it at the next opportunity. Good luck, Chief. Semper Paratus."

"Semper Paratus, Sir."

By late September the *Northland* had the responsibility to escort a large convoy into the Russian port of Murmansk. Once that was accomplished they reversed their course and traveled at full speed due west toward the eastern coast of Greenland where they were scheduled to link up with the Coast Guard icebreaker *Eastwind*, which was breaking a channel from Rekjavik, Iceland, north up the coast to Cape Brewster where a small Norwegian and Danish contingent was operating a weather station. It was the final supply run for the next ten months when the ice froze deep enough so that the large icebreaker could not move. Scoresbysund was on the north shore of Cape Brewster. The Army had suggested that the *Northland* follow in their wake up to Scoresbysund where they could link up with their Eskimo sled drivers.

By the end of October the sun sets for three or four months of total darkness. The sun rises again towards the end of February. During the dark period, it is impossible for aircraft to see any-thing on the ground. Shadows and darkness made aerial reconnaissance useless. Thus the desire for the Allies to know for certain if the eastern coast north of Cape Brewster contained any German weather stations.

Ice was beginning to form on the open water making the demarcation between land and ocean difficult. The heavy *Eastwind* had begun breaking ice shortly out from Rekjavik. The *Northland* followed in their ice-littered trough. Nathan observed that large islands of icebergs that had been making their way southward were suddenly frozen in place like huge mountains of ice. Frequently the ice-breaker had to maneuver around some of the larger icebergs that often towered above them and were ten times as large as the vessel with two-thirds of their mass beneath their ice cover.

The small community known as Scoresbysund was nothing but a few buildings, one with a massive aerial antenna. The area around the settlement was only ice, snow, and desolation. Allied direction finders had hard evidence that a few scattered locations were sending signals in code. It could only mean that Germany had successfully established stations near the coast.

Nathan recalled his hesitation about the dangerous sledge patrols he had volunteered for. At the time he needed something more important than himself to help him forget about Shirley and the ultimate destruction of their marriage. He had volunteered for what could very well be a mission that he might not survive. He had looked around at his shipmates and hunched his shoulders. Every man participating in the war effort was facing that same potential for destruction. He never thought that his mission was any different.

Shirley was never far from his thoughts. They had known each other since the first grade. The thought that she was carrying another man's child in her body during his last furlough was repugnant to him. When he received word about her death, he had some reservations about their reconciliation. He thought she was sincere, but a gnawing remnant of disbelief kept giving him second thoughts. He felt guilty now. In his heart he desperately wanted to believe that Shirley's final act to cancel her unfaithfulness was in fact an act of love that they both shared. He needed that assurance to keep his sanity.

The crew of the *Northland* lined the rails, admiring the rugged landscape. Greenland defied its name by being nothing but a snow-blanketed land mass with rugged black and grey mountains towering close to the jagged coastline. Greenland is the world's largest island with a massive ice cap in places over two miles thick. Polar bear, walruses, fox, musk-ox, seals, and lemmings were the main inhabitants. Two thirds of the island was above the Arctic Circle.

Captain Andrews told Nathan that the Danish government had asked for assistance from the United States to protect the island. The primary agency responsible for that security was the Coast Guard who attached several of their high endurance cutters to the North Atlantic. Three months prior to the declaration of war by the United States, the Coast Guard had captured several German nationals who were operating a weather reporting station from the southern part of the eastern coastline. It had been a bold move in support of our British allies.

The eastern coast of Greenland is approximately sixteen hundred miles long. Nathan was informed that the ice-breaker could take them almost halfway up the coast, leaving about eight hundred miles for the patrol to cover. He had been told that a dog sled could travel an average of twenty miles per day which meant that they require a minimum of forty days one way if everything went as planned. The return trip would take equally as long. That meant that the patrol would be in the most demanding terrain in the world in the dead of winter for about three months. The further north they traveled, the more severe weather conditions became. Nathan began to wonder if he had made a mistake.

Airplanes had difficulty locating anything on the ground during the winter darkness. As a matter of fact, very few planes were capable of flying that far north at lower altitudes. The patrol would have to depend on the health and endurance of their sled dogs. That unknown made Nathan uncomfortable because he had no way of controlling anything about the dogs, the sleds, or the caliber of the Eskimo drivers.

The *Eastwind* signaled that they were approaching their rendezvous at Scoresbysund. Nathan joined Captain Andrews on the bridge of the cutter, anxious to check out the landing area. The days were getting shorter with visibility getting less each passing day. The patrol team had only a few days before total darkness blanketed the area. There was an eerie stillness in the brisk air. The delineation between the Atlantic Ocean and the landmass was indistinguishable except for large cracks in the ice formations close to the shoreline.

In the distance they could detect movement on the ice cap. Several dog teams were traveling towards the two ships. Captain Andrews turned toward Nathan. "Are you and your team ready for your great adventure, Chief?"

He stared at the approaching sleds. "We're as prepared as can be expected, Sir. My, what a desolate scene. Nothing but ice and snow as far as the eye can see."

"I'll maneuver the cutter as close to the edge of the ice as possible so that you and your team can use the boarding stairs. You have a lot of equipment and supplies for the sledges that are available," Captain Andrews remarked, surveying the pile on the deck.

"The Army arctic experts have informed me that the supplies we need for a six or seven month patrol will be adequate provided we supplement our food supply with whatever game is available," Nathan told him.

Nathan knew that the Danish Eskimos had already stocked dog food and fuel at several depots along the coast before the severe weather limited travel. The locations were about twenty miles apart and were well-marked on maps given to each of the Coast Guard team.

He assembled his team on the port side of the cutter ready to be transferred to the large platform of ice. He had watched them assemble with a satisfied smile. He had picked a fine bunch of young single men with a distinct yearning to take part in a unique adventure they could brag about in years to come to their grand-children. They were mesmerized by the unnatural semi-darkness and the silence of the scene before them.

Bob "Red" Allen spoke first. "Are those our dog teams approaching, Chief?" He was an expert radioman capable of dismantling them if necessary. Nathan had assigned him to be primarily responsible for the storage, packing and operation of radio and generating equipment. The equipment was heavy and awkward, but it was their only link to the outside world. Red was tall, lanky with a keen sense of humor. He was well-liked by his shipmates.

All of the Coasties were good team players. Little did Nathan realize on that first day just how important each man was to the successful completion of the mission. Their bond of friendship defied definition and would last a lifetime. The other three members, Chuck Murdock, Leo Mann and Barry Perkins were all from northern Maine where they experienced harsh winters on an annual basis. Chuck, a powerful high school football player, became the team's favorite cook. Leo and Barry were the team's best skiers. All had enjoyed hunting, fishing, and hiking before joining the Coast Guard.

Captain Andrews ordered the supplies and equipment placed on the ice with a swinging boom. While that was taking place, the dog teams arrived, lining up their sleds next to the large mound of supplies. There were five sleds, each with an

Eskimo driver. Nathan was surprised at their relatively small stature. They were barely five feet tall, but they were muscular and agile.

An official from the Danish Colonial government weather station at Scoresbysund accompanied the five sleds. Hans Jessup, a serious man with bright blue eyes, spoke English and hailed Captain Andrews. "Ahoy, Captain. I've come to introduce you to the sled drivers I have selected for our joint venture."

Captain Andrews saluted him and called out, "Our team leader is Chief Nathan Collins. He's coming down the ladder now."

Jessup met Nathan as he stepped onto the ice. "I'm Hans Jessup, Chief Collins. We are pleased that the United States has joined us in this operation. I think you'll approve my choice of drivers. They'll follow your orders without question, but I suggest that you listen to any advice they may offer. They have lived and survived in this harsh environment and are expert dog handlers. Come, let me introduce you."

Nathan shook his hand and introduced the Coasties. The five Eskimos had lived in several different locations in northern Greenland. Jessup spoke to two of the men in their native language. Their names were Mathew and John. Three of the men, Peter, Paul and Luke, spoke English. The Coasties and Eskimos shook hands and privately evaluated each other.

Nathan met each man with a smile. "The books of the New Testament are well represented here. I look forward to conducting this mission with such seasoned men. We plan to carry it out in a spirit of cooperation. If I step out of bounds, please let me know. Me and my men will rely on your expertise and experience in your vast homeland."

One of the sled drivers, Paul, smiled easily and shook hands with a graceful enthusiasm. "I have been selected to act as spokesman for the drivers. We are honored to receive your assistance and will do everything possible to bring this mission to a successful ending. We have two rifles with us which we will use for hunting. We are not soldiers and will rely on you and your men to confront any Germans we may encounter. Our government has asked us to not resist the enemy. Do you understand our position?"

Slightly confused with what Paul had told him, Nathan asked, "Will you back us up in a confrontation if it becomes necessary?"

"Yes, and we will defend ourselves, too."

Jessup explained, "What Paul is trying to say is that if the Germans knew that the native population was resisting their presence, then they would brutally retaliate against them when they are relatively unable to defend themselves. This is a harsh land. The Governor of Greenland had ordered all free men to come south of Scoresbysund. That way any people found north of that point could safely be considered German agents."

Nathan's orders were to destroy or capture any individuals they encountered north of Scoresbysund. It was impressed on him that Greenland could be a valuable stepping stone to Europe for the United States. The Germans recognized that potential and had sent many weather station operatives into the region. Weather was a vital link to military operations.

Coasties rushed to assist in loading the supplies. The native drivers protested that they wanted to do the loading. They let it be known that loading the sled required special attention to dispersing food, fuel, blankets, and tents equally throughout the sleds in case one of them was lost in a wide crevasse slightly covered with snow or from sinking in an area of thin ice. Red Allen impressed upon the drivers that the radio and generator were the most valuable pieces of equipment.

Peter smiled at Red, "Then the radio will be placed on my sled. I have the fastest and strongest team."

Each of Nathan's team was issued a pair of skis. They were outfitted with a fur-lined cap with a pair of goggles and heavy sheep-skin parkas with a fur-lined hood. They carried their M-1 rifles in slings across their backs with several ammo clips in their pockets. Each had a knife on their right leg inserted into their boots. It was standard Army arctic issue. The Eskimos wore a loose fitting sealskin coat with a fur-lined hood and sealskin boots covering up over their knees.

The Coasties noted that the Eskimos carried their personal supplies on a flat sled hauled behind one of the sleds. Paul turned to the Coasties saying, "We call this an ahkio, you would call it a toboggan."

An hour later, the sleds were loaded with all of their equipment and secured to Nathan's satisfaction. The dogs were harnessed in the shape of a fan for travel over the large flat ice mass into Cape Brewster over a hundred miles. Paul told them that it was faster than if the dogs were harnessed in tandem which was the preferred method in snow and rough terrain.

Nathan fastened his skis and turned for one last look at the *Northland.* It was a beautiful ship and he felt a pang of apprehension that he was leaving its security for the vast unknown. Captain Andrews was leaning against the rail and saluted him. Nathan returned the salute and shoved off into the Arctic North.

Chapter Eight

Arctic Patrol – 1943

A cool breeze swept across Nathan's face as he sat on the rocky shore remembering how it had been in years past. His twenty years of service in the Coast Guard had been filled with excitement. He had enjoyed the camaraderie of his shipmates and had established several long-lasting friendships which had continued after his retirement. The Coast Guard had been his refuge from domestic life which never seemed to work well for him. His first wife Shirley had died under grotesque circumstances while undergoing an abortion of another man's child. It had taken him a long time to recover from that trauma.

Now in looking back at his reaction to the incident, he had been reckless and uncaring about himself. Though he had volunteered for the arctic patrol of 1942 partially to help him forget his personal troubles on the home front, that operation had lifted him from the depths of a depression to the stark reality that he had placed himself and his men in a dangerous situation. His thoughts frequently returned to that fateful day when the Greenland patrol left the safety of the *Northland* for the endless ice and snow plateau that rose abruptly from the rock-strewn coastline.

The desolate Arctic is a dangerous place for those hardy individuals who enter its domain unprepared for its uncompromising severity. The universal struggle is to stay alive. Climate is the common enemy of man and beast. Those who adapt to its reality and who accept their own mortality frequently find peace and harmony in its breathtaking beauty.

A true feeling of freedom slowly creeps into man's consciousness once he has severed the shackles of structured society. A deep sense of respect and achievement fills those who have survived the howling winds and temperatures minus fifty degrees Centigrade.

Watching the outline of the *Northland* disappear behind them was not easy for the Coasties. It instantly brought them to the reality that they were alone in a strange land with strangers guiding them. It had given Nathan some pause, but the cheerfulness and confidence of the Eskimo sled drivers eased his worries. His gut had told him that they were in competent hands the moment he met the resourceful Inuits who lived and thrived in the environment they were now entering.

The winter of 1942-43 was the most memorable period of Nathan's life. The five intrepid Coastguardsmen followed behind the five dogsleds at a faster pace than they could walk. The ice was smooth with a light dusting of loose snow. After two hours at a brisk pace the Eskimos drivers turned north, leaving the flat span of ice for the undulated section of jagged ice formations near the coastline of Cape Brewster's northern shore. A high precipitous mountain range loomed off to their left. They encountered broken fissures in the ice the closer they came to the shoreline. The point where ocean ice meets the more stable land formations is the most treacherous for travel. At this juncture, the traveler must be alert for crevices that are large enough to swallow a man or a dogsled.

Paul motioned for everyone to stop. The dogs traveled a short distance and stopped in place. "We are going to change the dogs into a tandem harness for the rough section of ice ahead. We can all use a little rest. You men have done well to keep abreast of the dogs. The coastal fjords with their easy access to the ocean in the few weeks of summer are the most likely locations for the Germans to locate a weather station. They may even use a ship that has been frozen in place for the winter as a base of supply. We're going to set a slower pace from now on. Do you have any questions, Chief?"

Nathan rested on his poles and said, "Our mission is to secure and evaluate the coastal region, Paul. It is unlikely that enemy agents will travel very far inland to establish a station. I agree with your assessment and will rely on your judgment."

"The dogs are our most valuable ally here in the Arctic. They can detect a human a mile away and will generally turn towards them without direction from the driver. We can tell when they have a scent. They bark vigorously for either man or beast such as a wolf or a polar bear. Usually they stand in place when they detect a bear," Paul told them.

"Are bears a problem, Paul?" Red Allen asked.

"Polar bears require due diligence. They are curious and ferocious. The dogs will always let us know when bears are nearby, even if they have been sleeping soundly. Dogs fear the bear. We sleep with a rifle close by."

"What kind of rifle do you use, Paul?" asked Nathan curiously.

"We have two Enfield .303 bolt action rifles. They are the same the British Army use. As soon as we harness the dogs we'll proceed at a more cautious rate. Matthews is our best tracker and will lead us in single file. If any of you tire you can hitch a ride behind one of the sleds," Paul suggested, aligning his team of huskies in a single file.

"It'll take a while to get into shape. You lead, and we'll follow, Paul."

Sheer cliffs ten thousand feet tall along the shoreline have a pinkish hue with streaks of green and gray lichen growing along the seams. Matthew selected a trail through canyons of ice and jagged rock formations with an uncanny eye for terrain that Nathan soon learned to respect. Wind velocity increased as soon as they began the climb from the coastal plateau. Loose snow blew constantly from one place to another. The arctic rarely has heavy snow accumulation. When the winds are heavy the snow crystals can sting the skin, making face masks a must for prolonged exposure.

The patrol pushed northward crossing numerous fjords. The area was dotted with small ice-covered islands close to the mainland coast. The protected canyons and inlets were ideal locations for the establishment of a winter weather station. The weather was consistently foggy and cold. It was rare when they could see more than a few hundred feet beyond their line of travel. During this initial period of their patrol Nathan and the Coasties developed a trust and respect for their Eskimo companions. They were born to this land. Generations of survival in the most hazardous climate in the world had developed skills and awareness that the white outsider could never duplicate.

The second day of their patrol they were alerted to something unusual. The dogs had heard or smelled something ahead of them that aroused their curiosity and they began to race towards the east along the shoreline with an ice covered inlet. Nathan was being pulled by the lead dog team. The surrounding area was an ideal location for a station. The high ground sheltered it from the winds. Using his binoculars, Nathan located an antennac rising above one of the cliffs, instantly motioning for them to stop. He unslung his rifle and checked to see that the action was not frozen, and turned to face the men behind him.

"I can see what I believe is an antenna ahead of us. What do you think, Paul?"

"The dogs have picked up something unusual. If you see an antenna then we have to assume that it is an enemy installation," Paul replied calmly. "All of our Danish stations are south of us."

"We should approach the location without the dogs," Nathan suggested. "Paul, you and your drivers should find a good spot to hide the dogs and sleds. We'll continue on skis to reconnoiter the area, then we'll plan an attack. I've been thinking about our situation. What do we do if we take prisoners?"

"Let's worry about that when we have to," exclaimed Red, checking his rifle.

Nathan studied his map. It appeared to him that the best strategy was to flank or surround any structure they may find. Paul and his drivers pulled off the trail into an enclave that adequately hid the dogs and sleds from view. They continued several hundred feet on skis when they saw the roof of a shack nestled among the rocks. Nathan directed them to remove the skis and to take positions around the building. Visibility was limited by a rolling fog bank that blanketed the area. That gave them a greater sense of security. The enemy could not see them. Nathan used the fog to rapidly advance closer to the shack.

So far they saw and heard nothing from the shack. If they possessed dogs, they would alert the Germans to their presence. Hiding behind some rocks, Nathan motioned for the Coasties to come to him. From that vantage point they could see a guy wire for the antenna on higher ground opposite their location. The shack was readily visible with an outhouse about thirty feet away. The door was facing the frozen ocean.

He pointed out the positions for each of the men and slowly began to work his way around the building until he could see the door. He took a position behind some rocks where he could observe the entrance and checked to see that the men were in position around the cabin. Suddenly the door opened and a man raced to the outhouse and entered. That was a good sign, thought Nathan. They had not been discovered.

If he knew how many men were inside, he'd crash the door and take them by surprise. Then, he raised the Garand and placed three shots into the smoke stack above the shack and shouted: "Achtung, Achtung. We are Americans, come out of the cabin with your hands up. You are surrounded."

The man in the outhouse rushed toward the shack. Nathan fired at the ice in front of the man and ordered him to stop with hands in the air. The man saw Nathan standing with a rifle at his shoulder and did as he was ordered. Nathan ran to him, making him lie face down on the ice with hands placed at the small of his back.

Just then the door crashed open and a fusillade of shots echoed from inside the shack. Nathan ran towards the outhouse emptying his rifle with four more shots at the door, quickly thrusting a fresh ammunition clip into the Garand. Up to that point his men had not fired a shot. Nathan hollered, "Okay men, two shots each into the cabin. They need some persuasion."

Ten rounds entered the cabin from different directions. Moments later two men walked out with their hands up.

"Come in closer," Nathan called out to the Coasties, and lowered his rifle towards the Germans. "Do any of you Germans speak English?"

The man lying on the ground answered, "Yes, I speak English."

"How many men are in the building?"

"There are four of us."

"Tell them to lie down like you. Where's the fourth person?" Nathan continued questioning the man.

"He has been sick and is in his bunk. You have wounded two of the men," answered the one on the ground.

Nathan called for the Coasties to come in and secure the area. The Germans were shaken to see the four Coastguardsman checking the outhouse and the shack thoroughly. Red Allen was especially interested in their radio equipment. Nathan entered the cabin to see that it was heated by a centrally located kerosene stove. He was most interested in checking the sick man. He noted a set of four bunks against the far corner of the shack and approached it cautiously. He saw a man lying on the bottom bunk staring at him.

"I am a chief petty officer in the United States Coast Guard. We have surrounded your cabin. You are our prisoners. Your friend told me that you are ill? Do you understand what I'm saying?" Nathan asked, checking the man's brow for a temperature.

The man was frightened by the presence of American military at their secluded location. He shook his head. "I understand you. My name is Franz. I am not a soldier. I have been sick for two days, vomiting anything that I eat."

Nathan was concerned for the weakened sick man running a fever. Chuck and Leo assisted the two men lying on the ice into the cabin. Red reported that he had checked the diesel powered generator located in the outhouse. Nathan left the cabin and fired three shots into the air with his .45 pistol to signal the Eskimos to join them. A few minutes later, the sleds circled around the cabin. Paul approached Nathan who described their situation. Two of the Germans had minor wounds which were being treated by the Coasties with help from a very well equipped German first aid kit.

Nathan took Paul aside and spoke in hushed tones. "The sick man needs medical care, Paul. We can't leave him here either. I've been thinking of a plan to transport all four of the Germans to Scoresbysund. What do you think?"

Paul was reluctant at first, but the logic of their situation could not be denied. "This is a very well equipped station, Chief. It could be very useful to us. Two sleds could be used to transport the men back to Scoresbysund. We'd have to trim the food supplies to the minimum."

"Will your men be comfortable with the responsibility, Paul?"

"If we keep them well secured, they won't be a problem. If they become difficult we can simply threaten to leave them alone on the ice without food or shelter. The dogs will only answer to the driver's commands. I notice that the Germans are not wearing any uniforms."

Nathan returned to the cabin where the Germans were sitting on the floor tied together in a corner. The Coasties were heating water on the stove for coffee and tea. "Are you Germans soldiers or civilians?" Nathan demanded.

Franz quickly answered, "We are civilian technicians."

Paul entered the cabin to announce that he had selected two sleds to make the run back to Scoresbysund. "The two drivers should be armed with side arms for protection and security. They will be tied to the sleds for the duration of the trip without exception, even if they have to stop for rest. Two of my best companions are fully capable of making the trip without sleep. They could sleep at the base camp before joining us to resume our patrol."

"I could not ask for more, Paul. Thank your men for us. We'll hold up here at the cabin until our friends return. Perhaps they can bring a Danish crew back with them to operate this facility."

Chapter Nine

Arctic Patrol, 1943

Red Allen spent a couple of hours familiarizing himself with the German's radio setup. It was a fine piece of technology with much greater power than the portable transmitter still packed on one of the sledges outside of the cabin.

"Hey, Chief!" Red exclaimed with glee, "I've got Scoresbysund on the line. What do you want me to say to them?"

"Tell them to be on the lookout for our sledges with the German prisoners, which we are dispatching now as we speak. Ask them if they have any more intelligence for us?"

"Will do, Chief."

Twenty minutes later, Red informed Nathan that the base station was still getting radio static from some station north of the one they had just captured. They were sending in a code that the Danes had not broken. They only knew that another station was frequently operating at all times of the day or night, indicating that it must be well-staffed.

Nathan had discussed it with Paul. "Do you have any idea where the other station might be, Paul?"

"I've traveled the full length of the east coast twice in the past two years. I have not seen or heard of any such facility. A very large station could easily be nestled within one of the coves or fjords and would never be seen unless you happen to stumble on it by chance. Sorry, Chief Collins," Paul reluctantly replied, knowing that Nathan was disappointed.

That night, they all slept inside the cabin except for a sentry posted outside for security. Actually the evening hours were the same as during the day. One had to eat, sleep, and work by the clock instead of the natural rhythm in the lower latitudes. It required discipline that the Coasties had not mastered yet. They still expected to see the sun rise out of the east. Now the only source of light were the stars, the moon, and the magnificent phenomenon of the northern lights. They streaked across the galaxy like electronic lines of red, orange, blue and yellow erratically marking up the dark void between the stars.

Three days after the task force escorted the German prisoners to safety, Nathan and Red Allen could hear the barking of dogs in the distance. The other members of the team were scouting the terrain in more detail a few miles north of the cabin. The returning team, Peter and Matthew, pulled their sledge to a stop in front of the cabin. They were all smiles. They had successfully carried out a very delicate mission even though they had slept very little. Nathan congratulated them and insisted that they come inside to eat and to rest.

Peter held up his hands. "First, we must care for the dogs. We'll secure them for a well-earned rest and give them an extra ration of food. We have a satchel of dispatches for you, Chief."

Nathan accepted the leather pouch and rushed inside to check the contents, directing Red to heat water for Matthew and Peter so that they could enjoy a hot tea. Sitting at the crude table with a lantern overhead, Nathan sorted a packet of mail for each of them. A note was attached to his bundle of three letters. He anxiously read:

Dear Chief Collins;

A note in haste for your sledge drivers to carry back to you. We are pleased with the German prisoners. They told us that the other station is about sixty miles north of your current location. It is manned by 8 or 10 German soldiers. Use caution when approaching their facility. Your main mission is to eliminate transmission of weather information to the German high command. Do not attempt to confront a larger force unless you are absolutely certain of success. It is only necessary to destroy their capacity to transmit... Good luck.

Hans Jessup

Included in the packet were two letters one from his mother and father and another from Shirley's sister, Lena Moore. He opened the letter from Lena with interest.

Searsport, Maine

December 5, 1942

Dear Nathan,

We do not know where you are, but you must know that we are with you in spirit. You are always in our prayers. My heart went out to you when your parents told me about Shirley. It was bad enough for us to handle, but I cannot imagine what a terrible thing it was for you to accept. We are hoping that the Coast Guard will grant you some leave time and send you home. They may yet do that.

The war has been raging for a year now. The world is tearing itself apart. I recently received word that my fiancée, and your best friend, Don Murray has been killed in action. His destroyer was lost somewhere in the Pacific with very few survivors. I'm still having a hard time reconciling the fact that he is not coming home. My God, there's no end to the misery and suffering caused by the war.

Casey stayed with me over this past weekend. Your folks both had bad colds and did not want to pass it on to him. For a two-and-a-half-year-old, he's very active and bright. He asks about you a lot and can point to the North Atlantic on my globe. Shirley would be proud of him, I'm sure.

Your folks told us that you are stationed in the North Atlantic. We are now experiencing a strong "northeaster" blowing drifts everywhere. I can't imagine how terribly cold it must be where you are. Our thoughts are always with you, dear Nat. Your family awaits your return with strained optimism. May the North Star guide you in your travels and may the good Lord keep you safe from harm.

Love, Lena

Nathan carefully folded the letter and placed it back in the envelope. Looking about the small cabin, he noted that each of the men were engrossed in the precious letters from home. They were by far the most simple and most effective ingredient in maintaining high morale. Sober reflections of happier times and places were a refreshing interlude in the dangerous cat-and-mouse game they were playing. Word from home allowed each of them to escape for a hallowed moment from the vast expanse of ice that made up Greenland. Those intimate moments made their sacrifices worthwhile.

Using a pencil (ink in a pen froze solid in the Arctic) to answer letters from Lena and his parents, he thanked them for the prayers in the flickering light of an alcohol lamp. He could not tell them where he was or what he was doing, but it was important that he assure them that he was doing just fine.

In his haste to reply he had overlooked a small envelope addressed to him in care of his parents. It was from Dr. Mackey. He broke the seal and removed the single page with trembling fingers.

Wells, Maine

Christmas Day, 1942

Dear Chief Collins,

I'm sending this note to you in care of your folks in Belfast hoping they'll forward it to you. I made my final visit to check on a very young Coastie at the Wells barracks. The men told me that you had been selected for some special mission in the North Atlantic.

I'm leaving Wells. I've been offered a commission in the Army Medical Corps. My baby girl, Cora, will be well cared for by my folks in Monson, Maine. It's time that I made a more direct contribution to the war effort. I have received word from the Army that Donald was a casualty of the evacuation of Bataan. It has influenced my decision to join the Army. Perhaps I can find some consolation in serving our brave soldiers.

As I leave Wells, I fondly remember all the friends who made my time here so special, and that includes you, Nathan. Your Christmas gift will always be a reminder of our friendship. May our prayers spin a cocoon of armor around you and keep you safe.

Good-bye dear friend,

Colleen Mackey

The letter had ignited a spark that was always deep within his conscience. Memories of fleeting moments with the gentle doctor never failed to make him melancholic. The warmth of their last parting was only a miniscule moment in time, yet it endured and grew over the months since he left the states. Those memories were a source of comfort and of self-loathing, for she was a married woman carrying another man's child. To harbor feelings beyond that of friendship was potentially self-destructive. He was fully aware of that, but the friendly note dredged up the dormant feelings that ran wild through his thoughts that night. Sleep came slowly.

The Coasties were still having trouble adapting to the continuous darkness that defined the winter months of the Arctic four hundred miles north of the Arctic Circle. Their internal clocks were guided by darkness and sunshine instead of the sameness of partial darkness. Most covered their heads with blankets but usually sleep came from physical exhaustion rather than from an arbitrary time table.

The morning after the return of Matthew and Peter, the patrol vacated the cabin, continuing their trek northward. Instead of making a straight line inland of the coast. They had decided to move on the frozen ocean ice pack so that they could examine the numerous fjords and inlets along the way. Cracks in the ice pack at the juncture of the coast and ocean could be more dangerous a little later in the season, but for the time being it was more than sufficient to support the heavy sledges.

The unanimous opinion was that any German weather station had to be established and supplied from the sea; therefore, it would be close to a sheltered inlet or cove that was accessible by ocean-going vessels. Powerful radio equipment could have been dropped by air, however, the drivers all stated vigorously it was a rarity to see an airplane.

For several days, the dog teams guided the patrol up and down lonely fjords devoid of human activity. On occasion they saw musk-ox and polar bears in the distance. They were usually sensed by the dogs before humans could see them. The bears made the dogs nervous and they were content to lead the sledges away from them in a frenzied dash.

Peter and Paul announced to Nathan the need for dog food replenishment. If the opportunity arrived, they should shoot a polar bear or musk-ox. They had seen a lot of sign of polar bear activity and cautioned everyone to be alert for a possible visitation. Peter assured the Coasties that the dogs would forewarn them if a bear approached their bivouac.

Near the midnight hour, the compact campsite erupted in a cacophony of dogs barking, yelping and howling in fear. A bear had invaded their space and was swatting the dogs about as if they were basket balls.

The team had kept the dogs in their harnesses for the night to insure that they did not run away in case of an attack. Some of the dogs were so aroused by the bear's presence that they broke free of the harnesses and ran away from the scene.

Nathan and Red Allen were the first to break out of their tent, rifles in hand, to see the bear actually eating one of the dogs they had killed. The Eskimos insisted in camping within the circle of dogs and sledges. That way any bear visiting them had to contend with the dogs first. Surprisingly, Nathan and Red surveyed the scene and calmly kneeled to fire at the bear. Two rounds from each of their Garands brought the bear down. Each round found their mark in the head and upper torso of the animal. They waited to make sure the bear was dead before approaching it. The dogs were whipped to a high frenzy, requiring all the skills of the drivers to settle them down so that they could assess the damage wreaked on their campsite on an open ice field.

Paul cautiously approached the bear, placing a round from his Enfield rifle into the animal's mouth. He turned towards Nathan to announce, "He is dead!"

Nathan joined the drivers to calm the dogs. Four of them were dead and had to be removed from their harness. Three dogs had severed their harness and were nowhere in sight. "They will return," Paul stated, "They are governed by hunger the same as the bear and will come back to us when they have exhausted their fear of the polar bear. They know where the next meal comes from."

The entire team was now checking the sledges and the supplies. Several had been overturned in the melee. One sledge had a broken runner beyond repair. It had gotten caught in a fissure in the ice while the team tried to pull it sideways. It was a serious loss.

The drivers immediately began to dress the bear, first carving out bite-size pieces for the dogs. They were fed until they could not eat any more. They then cut the remaining meat into thin steaks. Two thirds of the bear meat was processed for dog food. Choice steaks were cooked for their next meal. The Coasties enjoyed the steaks comparing them to pork, except the bear meat was tenderer.

That night, after feasting on bear steaks and dehydrated mashed potatoes, Paul approached Nathan with a report. "We have lost four dogs dead; three have run away, but they will return soon. One sledge is out of commission as far as the patrol is concerned. I suggest we send it back to the cabin. A driver can negotiate the more level ice fields with one runner broken. The sledge can be dragged with one runner. We could equip the sledge with enough food for one man to make the trip. We'll harness the injured dogs to the broken sledge."

"Can we carry enough supplies on the four sledges to accomplish our mission, Paul?" Nathan asked. "I'm not concerned for us as much as I am for the man who has to make the trip alone."

"We can alert the base camp that he is on his way. They will send out a party to look for him if he has not shown up in a reasonable length of time. We are capable of surviving with adequate food. I have faith that my man will be able to make the trip alone."

The decision bothered Nathan. The driver's safety was his responsibility. They were several day's travel out from the cabin. "Can any of you operate the radio at the German cabin we just left?"

Paul frowned and replied, "I am the only one who has some experience with radios. Maybe your radioman, Red, can instruct John how to use it."

"I was just thinking," Nathan added. "We could call Scoresbysund to send out a patrol to the German weather station. Once they arrive they could call us. By then John would be somewhere close by. If he has not shown up we could give them a compass bearing John was using."

Paul was pleased with the suggestion. "Your concern for the man who leaves us is appreciated, Chief. What you say is the correct way to handle it."

All parties agreed that they would remain at their present location long enough to prepare the broken sledge for the journey. Red and Chuck set up the radio and generator in their tent. Chuck manned the cranking handles on the generator. The extreme cold temperatures congealed the lubricants on the bearings making it very difficult to move. Chuck was the strongest man in the team and even he had trouble turning the handles fast enough to generate power to transmit the message Red wanted to send. The first few turns were almost impossible. Chuck was afraid he might break one of the handles. He told Red to turn up the alcohol stove to maximum so that the heat could soften the lubricants. A half hour later, he was able to rotate the generator to get out the message.

That evening, the drivers had secured the dogs and packed the meat on the sledges. Nathan was anxious to continue their patrol in the morning. John had already departed for the cabin. Scoresbysund had informed them a crew was underway for the cabin, and a well-equipped sledge patrol was ordered to intercept John with the broken sledge. Everyone was relieved to receive the news.

Shortly after the exhausted men had retired to their heated tents, two sentries, Chuck and Peter, alerted the camp that two polar bears could be seen in the distance. They were prepared to shoot the bears once they came closer to the camp so that they could place their shots with precision.

Nathan quickly joined the two men. "Where are the bears?" he asked, fastening his parka.

"Off to our east, Chief," Chuck pointed to two dark moving objects. The dogs were noticeably less vocal than they had been with the earlier bear confrontation.

"Perhaps the dogs are more fearful than yesterday," Peter shook his head. "It is right that we post all night sentries."

Without warning the two bears increased their speed and charged the campsite. The scent of fresh blood erased any caution they might have used. It was amazing how fast they could travel. Nathan wiped the frost crystals from his eyelids and eyebrows. He had left his face mask in the tent. "Steady now," he calmly spoke, raising his rifle.

"We should not let them get too close to the perimeter," Peter warned. "At a hundred feet we should fire."

The still arctic air resonated to the sound of gunfire as all three shooters fired a round each at the galloping bears. To their dismay, the smaller bear howled and rolled to one side sliding along on the ice. The larger bear continued without flinching. The three fired another round each into the enraged animal. The shots seemed to anger him instead of stopping him.

Nathan was standing behind a sledge filled with meat which was the destination for the bear. They were all dismayed at the animal's ability to absorb so much punishment. Chuck, in desperation, emptied the balance of his five bullets into the charging bloody hulk. Nathan's rifle had a misfire. He hesitated a moment to extract the cartridge by hand when the bear crashed into him. The crazed animal swept him into his powerful arms knocking him backwards!

Chapter Ten

Chuck dropped his empty rifle and leaped on the back of the polar bear, falling to the ground with Nathan still in his grip. Chuck placed a powerful left arm around the bear's head, lifting it to prevent the animal from biting Nathan and drove his razor sharp seaman's knife deep across the bear's throat almost decapitating him. The bear tried desperately to shake Chuck off his back, all the while making gurgling sounds with blood streaming from his mouth.

Leo Mann was late in coming to the scene where he saw Chuck and Nathan closely intertwined with the beast. Drawing his .45 pistol, Leo fired three shots into the bear's open mouth. Slowly the animal fell to the ground taking Nathan and Chuck with him.

Peter was prepared to place another round into the bear's head. "Are you all right, Chief?"

Nathan was sitting on the ground trying to dislodge his leg from the dead weight of the bear. He replied, "I think so, Peter, frightened but unharmed. That was some quick thinking, Chuck. You took an awful chance wrestling with a bear."

Chuck cleaned the blood off his knife in the snow. "I figured that all the lead he had absorbed had taken some of the fight out of him. Wow, what a smelly breath he had."

"I was too scared to notice," Nathan stated soberly, wiping the blood from his face and chest.

Peter carefully examined the bear to make sure he was dead. "We have more meat than we can carry."

"For now," Nathan explained, "I'm going to clean up. We should try to rest. Tomorrow will be a busy day getting underway. I'm anxious to continue our patrol."

"Should we process any meat, Chief?" Peter asked.

"If we can't take it with us we should not waste time on the carcass. I know it's a shame to waste food, but there's nothing we can do about it."

"Whatever you say, Chief," Peter quietly answered, shaking his head at the waste of a fine animal.

Three days of traveling twelve to fourteen hours per day, they covered over sixty miles in and around inlets and fjords always pushing northward into colder and more severe weather conditions. The area required constant vigilance. Exposed skin froze in minutes. Even with face masks to protect them, all of the Coasties experienced frostbite on their faces. Eye lashes and long beards collected frost icicles that interfered with their vision and breathing. Goggles helped even though they frequently fogged up, blinding them.

At night, each man curled up on a sealskin mat provided by the Eskimos. It helped to insulate them from the ice. Their small alcohol stoves were capable of heating their tents up to sixty degrees while they cooked their meals and heated snow for hot tea. Without the warm tents, the men honestly believed that they could not have survived in the vicious and unrelenting weather. The warm tents allowed them to dry their boots and socks. Every man slept with their rifles beneath the blankets. They never forgot the ferocity of an unprovoked polar bear attack.

At the end of the third day after the bear encounter, they took shelter in a cave near the shoreline. It had been used as a shelter by others and was clearly marked on their maps. The cave was large enough for all of the sleds and dogs. The party was glad to conserve their alcohol fuel by starting several small coal fires on rocky foundations built for that purpose. The fires were a little smoky, but the coal fires soon heated the cave enough that they could dry their boots and socks and quickly change into clean underwear. They all joked about how they would be rejected by polite socialites in their present status. The cold penetrated all of their garments enough that even when they were physically stressed, they rarely worked up a sweat.

That night, Nathan slept more soundly within the snug confines of the cave than he had experienced in their tents on the open ice fields exposed to the incessant winds and threats of polar bear invasions. The ubiquitous howling winds whistled past the opening in the cave, sucking out the smoke from the coal fire. Even so, Nathan had grown used to sleeping with his head under the cover of blankets and fur skins so that he could breathe easier. It also gave him a greater sense of privacy in his small cocoon.

Thoughts of home, especially Casey, dominated his evening remembrances. He was saddened that his son was growing up without a mother to care for him. The long absences of his father were a source of guilt and longing. The consuming isolation of the sledge patrol only added to his guilt. The latest letter Nathan received from Shirley's older sister, Lena, gave rise to several small incidents that took place while they attended high school.

Nathan and his best friend, Dan Murray, had often gone out on double dates with Shirley and Lena to the movies and to school dances. One Saturday in late July 1936, the couples had pedaled their bicycles to the small annual fair at Belfast on the waterfront park. It was always a fun time with the added attraction of scary rides when they had enough money to spend on them. The highlight of the fair was the evening dance under the stars on the large pavilion. That year they were treated to a large full moon that highlighted the area. A full orchestra was made up of local talent including Nathan's mother, Avis, who played the piano.

Shirley and Nathan had danced all of the slow waltzes and fox-trots together. Shirley and Dan usually danced the faster tunes while Lena and Nathan sat and watched from the sidelines. Lena was a more serious and reflective person than her more out-going sister.

"Shirley told me that you'll be leaving for the Coast Guard soon," Lena had mentioned to him as they sat watching the dancers. "We'll miss you, Nathan."

"It's always nice to know that one will be missed," he had replied, noting a hesitant expression on her face. "The closer I get to the date I'm supposed to report for duty, the more I wonder if I made the right decision. I'm not certain what I want to do with my life. Perhaps a tour of duty in the Coast Guard will help to point me in the right direction. It's great that you'll be starting normal school this fall, Lena. We're all proud that you want to be a teacher."

"I was hoping that Shirley would join me when she graduates, but she has no interest in it," Lena had told him.

At the time he was surprised that Lena would add, "Shirley still has some growing up to do." Had she been trying to tell him something that beautiful moonlit night beside the dark Atlantic? He had reluctantly agreed with her, yet Shirley's bubbling personality and easy disposition were what had attracted him to her.

Lying beneath his sealskin cover, Nathan continued to recall how Lena had made a point of embracing him there on the platform of the train station when he left for the Coast Guard. She had held back, as was her way, until the two families had said their farewells and wished him good luck.

Just before he boarded the train, Lena had come into his arms to tell him, "We'll miss you more than you'll ever know, Nathan. Take care of yourself." She then kissed him on the cheek.

At the time, he thought little about her last-minute message. He and Shirley married shortly after the incident on his first furlough after boot camp. During one of their disagreements, Shirley had defiantly remarked: "Lena is in love with you."

He had quickly dismissed the accusation. Teenagers have traditionally thought that they were in love with a particular person. He himself had thought he was in love with other girls in high school. It was only puppy love and soon waned. Now, after receiving Lena's last letter he recalled that remark from Shirley and wondered…

At 2:00 AM Barry Perkins gently shook Nathan. "It's your turn for the morning shift, Chief. I left a pot of tea on the fire grate for you."

Nathan sat up to dress his feet with socks that had been drying on the rocks round the fire. "Thanks, Barry. It sounds as if the wind has picked up in velocity out there."

"It has, Chief. The aurora borealis is pretty active tonight. There's something about this lonely, desolate place that fascinates me. I thought I knew freedom back home, but up here, physical and emotional freedom is limitless. A person has to experience it to know how it affects us."

"Barry, you're a poet at heart," Nathan grinned.

The moment he climbed out of the cave to a position on top of their small knoll of coal, the wind began to penetrate the layers of clothing. He first checked his M1 to be sure that it could operate in the severe cold. They had found from experience that regular gun oil congealed and could jam the ejection mechanism in the minus 40 degree weather. As long as they kept the rifle mechanism dry it worked flawlessly, regardless of the temperature.

He watched in fascination the erratic designs of the northern lights around him. The humming and hissing sounds that emanated from the phenomenon was blanked out by the blizzard that swirled loose snow in and around every nook and crevice of the topography.

The still hours of darkness always held a fascination for him ever since he was a small boy. The semi-darkness that prevailed in the arctic latitudes had been interesting at first, but continuous darkness was too much. The openness of normal daylight was impersonal and presented all the world to those who took the time to see it. When darkness came, the environment became more intimate and personal. It encapsulated each person's own private world from prying eyes, making it a unique experience. Nathan was always able to better evaluate himself and his performances once the bright sun dipped below the horizon. Most of his important decisions were made in the soft hush of the evening.

He never found that same peace of mind in the arctic winter. The nights were too long, limiting vision and stifling dreams that normally flowed easily through his thoughts when the rest of the world slept.

Four hours after he took over the sentry station, Nathan returned to the welcome warmth of the cave to alert Red Allen for the final sentry duty of the day. He found him huddled around the fire drinking tea. He looked at Nathan with a frown. "We've got a problem, Chief."

"What's wrong, Red?"

"Barry has got a severe case of frostbite on his left foot. We've been wrapping it with warm water bottles and sealskin." Red stood up and grabbed his rifle prepared to take his turn on lookout.

Nathan kneeled beside Barry who had a pained expression on his face. "How long have you known about this, Barry?"

"I've had cold feet ever since the day we left the *Northland.* I didn't think anything about it until this morning when I came in from sentry duty to remove my boots and socks. My toes have been bleeding and I'm having trouble walking, Chief," Barry reluctantly told him. "I hate to be a problem. I was hoping that my feet would feel okay once they were completely warmed."

Nathan uncovered the wrappings around Barry's feet. They still had that grayish-yellow hue caused by frostbite. Once the skin was frozen, the tissue is very fragile and can be easily bruised causing excessive bleeding. He knew that the only cure was for Barry to remain warm and to drink plenty of liquids. For the time being he would have to stay off his feet. That created a problem for the patrol!

"You should have warned me that this was happening to you, Barry," Nathan remarked. "I'm not blaming you. Just rest easy and please keep warm. We'll come up with a solution. Semper Paratus."

"Semper Paratus, Chief. Maybe I can stay here in the cave until the patrol returns, then you could pick me up." Barry was concerned that he was a serious handicap to the successful completion of the mission.

Nathan was quick to snap back a reply. "No way, Barry. I'm not separating anyone from this patrol. Let me talk things over with the drivers. In the meantime, cover your feet, lay down on your sealskin, and rest. That's an order."

Everyone gathered around the fire to discuss their next move. Nathan had already concluded how they were going to handle Barry's situation. He suggested that they unload the supplies from one of the sledges and distribute it evenly among the remaining sledges to make room for Barry to be carried wrapped in several layers of skins and blankets sufficient to keep him warm. They could install one of their small heat-tab stoves beside Barry's foot so that the bleeding tissue could heal.

"If anyone has a better suggestion, I'll be glad to listen. One thing though, we do not leave any one alone. Any questions?"

No one objected to the proposal. Paul suggested that they try to find room to pack some of their foodstuff in and around Barry to keep it from freezing. A half hour later, they resumed their patrol with Barry nestled within a warm cocoon on the third sledge in the line of travel.

Red had joked that Barry looked quite comfortable in his new perch. "I may develop some illness if I can get the same treatment." They all laughed.

The patrol methodically checked every inlet along the shoreline for the next four days as they pushed deeper and deeper into the dark arctic night. Winds increased and temperatures steadily dropped with every mile they traveled. Nathan personally inspected every man's feet once they stopped for the night's rest. Barry was recuperating from his ordeal. On the third night, he insisted that he take a turn on his skis being pulled behind the sledge. Nathan admired his tenacity and warned him not to overdo on the first time out from his warm enclosure.

There was concern among the members that they might have missed the weather station that was still sending out reports. They were now several hundred miles from Scoresbysund and were approaching Shannon Island, a land mass several miles off the east coast of Greenland. Paul suggested that they make a complete circle around the icebound island. He was suspicious that their weather station might be within that sphere because it was normally the most northerly limit for ocean going vessels during the few weeks of summer. Nathan conceded to Paul's hunch.

Shannon was another large formation of granite and coal towering above a sea of ice. They continued to check small inlets and fjords as they slowly worked their way counterclockwise around the island. On the fifth day they knew that they were nearing the northern coast above the island. Nathan took the point position carefully scanning the terrain. Suddenly he stopped and motioned for Paul to come abreast of him. The train of sledges paused while the two men studied unnatural formations ahead.

Conversation was difficult in the harsh winds. Nathan cleaned the lens of his binoculars, scanning the area one more time. "You're correct, Paul," he screamed to be heard. "It looks to me like the radio antenna on the masts of a ship frozen into the ice. Your premonition was correct. We've found our German weather station!"

Chapter Eleven

Spring 1943

Each man in the sledge patrol breathed a sigh of relief that they had located the German station. They took shelter behind large granite formations south of the German ship so that they could adequately secure the sledges and dogs. Nathan studied the outline of the ship. Every inch of the vessel was covered with several inches of ice. He was impressed with the size of the vessel which housed the Germans. It had adequate mess and berthing facilities in a warm and secure structure. He had envied the creature comforts they enjoyed.

After studying the situation for a few minutes, he wondered if the estimated number of Germans could be correct. The ship was typical of the many small island supply vessels that plied the North Atlantic. It was about two hundred feet long and could be operated with a crew of twenty to thirty men. If that many men were on board, the sledge patrol had a problem on their hands!

"What do you think, Chief?" asked Red Allen, checking his side arm.

The wind was blowing harder than ever. It was difficult to be heard above the swirling blizzard. Nathan instructed Paul and Peter to take the sledges deeper into the cove and to set up the tents. The dogs should be fed extra rations to keep them quiet and contented. He informed the patrol that he was going to crawl closer to the ship to come up with some kind of tactic that would be successful. He directed Leo, Red, and Chuck to take positions where they could see the ship and at the same time be as invisible as possible.

He had everyone set their watches. It was now 3:00 PM. Nathan promised to be back by 9:00 PM with a plan of action, and hopefully with an estimate of how many troops they had to deal with. Before leaving the men, Nathan reminded them that they were to defend themselves in case they are discovered by alert German outposts. With that he disappeared in the swirling snow.

The ship had a steel hull and was wedged between two large icebergs that held the vessel upright like a vice. Nathan left his skis behind, taking advantage of an ice-covered rocky enclave that partially surrounded the ship. He sat on a vein of coal about a hundred feet from the ship's superstructure to study it from the elevated position. He noted that access to the deck from the irregular iceberg was possible over a wide gangplank with hand rails on the starboard side.

Ice several inches thick totally covered the superstructure except for one large chimney that protruded from the main deck close to the elevated bridge. Dark smoke was belching from it, indicating that they were burning coal for heat and had recently loaded the stove or furnace. He saw no evidence of outhouses, which meant that they were using the holding tanks on the ship. They probably started the main steam engines to empty the tanks once they were full. Nathan smiled. The German crew had the good sense to stay in their warm secured quarters, free of dependence on anything that would take them from their cocoon.

There was little evidence that he could see of the Germans utilizing any of the surrounding territory. However, Nathan knew that the Germans would post a lookout. Finding nothing, he secured his parka and face mask, settling down for a long vigil. At some point, they had to change the guard, and they most likely left the ship via the gangplank.

For two hours Nathan didn't move a muscle from his strategic location looking for movement of any kind. Finally, when every inch of his body throbbed from the cold and his feet were numb, he saw a figure walk out across the main deck off the bridge across the gangplank, disappearing below his line of sight. Several seconds later, a second man hurriedly retraced the steps back to the bridge through a door. Ah! His assumptions were correct. The main access to the ship was from the bridge!

Freshly armed with specific knowledge, Nathan left his perch stamping his feet as he briskly walked back to the base camp location. A plan was beginning to develop in his mind.

The plan was implemented early the next morning. Barry, Red, Leo, and Chuck were to accompany Nathan to the ice-embedded ship. He instructed Barry to take a position near where he had sat with a view looking down on the ship. Barry was the team's best shot. His mission was to eliminate any Germans who threatened the boarding party.

The plan was to stealthily approach the lone guard and eliminate him as a threat. Hopefully that could be accomplished without sounding any alarm. Chuck was given that task. The rest of the team circled to the starboard side of the ship opposite Barry's lookout position. The area was full of sharply pointed hillocks of ice. They afforded good cover for the boarding team. The sentry post was visible from their vantage point. It was a crude wooden crate standing on end to provide protection from the vicious winds that surrounded the area.

The guard carried a submachine gun. The team paused to give Chuck a chance to circle the guard post from its blind side to the north. The guard could view the entire ship and seemed to be indifferent to any threat from the north. The sledge patrol was a new development. Chuck left his rifle with Nathan relying on his sidearm and knife. He was able to climb around the wooden box cubicle unseen. Seconds later he confronted the guard who was too startled to speak. Chuck instinctively drove his knife into the enemy's chest while covering his mouth to prevent sounding any alarm.

With the sentry eliminated, the four Coasties ran across the gangplank to the bridge where they threw the fresh polar bear skin over the top of the chimney. They hoped the move would trigger a response from someone who would come out on the bridge to see why their quarters were filling with smoke.

Leo and Chuck, who had confiscated the sentry's submachine gun, covered the main door off the bridge. A minute later, two soldiers stepped out on the bridge. They were met with two pistols held to their heads. Nathan forced them off to one side of the bridge while Red covered the door.

"Do any of you speak English?" Nathan sternly demanded. "We're taking possession of your ship. You can do it peacefully without casualties, or you can be responsible for the death of your friends."

The German soldiers were lightly dressed in field uniforms. He looked for signs of rank and found none. One was an older man who studied the situation around him. He was not frightened by the pistol in the back of his head. "I understand some English." By then both men were shivering from the cold.

"How many men are below?" Nathan asked impatiently.

The man who spoke some English looked at the hide over the chimney. "I'll tell you what you want to know if you will remove the obstruction from the chimney. We have two very sick men below."

"We can do that. Now, how many men are below? Tell me before we remove the hide." Nathan demanded.

"We have a total of ten men in our group…"

Chuck reached over the rail of the bridge to yank the hide from the chimney.

"You and your friend are getting cold. I want you to order the crew up here on the bridge. The two sick men can remain below. If you try to pull any trick, you and your companion will die. We are the United States Coast Guard, and you are our prisoners. Now call your companions out. It's cold, and our trigger fingers are getting numb. Hurry!"

The elderly soldier shouted out a stern command. He was getting cold, and his lips were turning blue. Shortly, five men came running through the door. Two had Luger pistols in their hands. Nathan was concerned that the armed men were going to start a shootout there on the bridge. He quickly grabbed the German who spoke English, placing his pistol at his temple. "Tell them to throw their guns overboard, or you'll be the first casualty."

The soldier screamed hysterically for his companions not to resist. The two armed soldiers took several seconds to survey the situation. Chuck intentionally placed the submachine gun

91

under the chin of the second man to step through the bridge door. Nathan watched the younger of the two armed men. He had an arrogant sneer on his lips and was prepared to make a fight when his companion screamed hysterically for him to give up.

The last minute confrontation ended with a sigh of relief when the Germans threw their pistols over the side. Nathan told Chuck to stay alert on the bridge and motioned for the remaining men to follow him through the door. They entered a large room insulated with thick pieces of cork attached to the steel hull of the ship. Nathan assumed that it was the Captain's quarters now being used for storage of food and other supplies. He ordered the Germans to form a circle with their backs to each other so that they could be tightly roped together.

Nathan had left his rifle on the bridge and was using his pistol in the close quarters. He took the arm of the German who spoke English, fastening a pair of handcuffs on him. "Now take me to the two sick men."

The man pointed to a pair of steps lit by a kerosene lantern to an open hold normally used for storage of freight. He quickly surveyed the area. It had been converted into a berthing and mess area combined. The large hold was warm and bright with lights placed all around the bulkhead. There was a large coal stove placed at the center of the room with hundreds of bags of coal neatly piled in a corner.

The radio room was off the kitchen facilities. Nathan checked to see if anyone was in the room. It was equipped with a powerful communication system. He then turned to his main concern. "Tell me what's wrong with the sick men?"

One of the sick men, Hugo Breyman, was a civilian who had been forced to take the assignment as a radio technician for their duration in Greenland. He spoke some English.

Nathan kneeled down to speak to him. "How do you feel, Mr. Breyman?"

He had a pale complexion. "I believe I have an inflamed appendix. No matter what I eat, it makes me sick," Breyman answered. There was fear in his eyes. Both he and Nathan knew that if it ruptured, his time was limited. His chances of waiting for spring thaw was unlikely at best.

"I am an American Coast Guard chief petty officer. You are our prisoners, and that makes us responsible for your care," Nathan told him, rising to check the condition of the second patient who had fallen on the ice while on sentry duty. He had a broken leg and was unable to move on his own.

Nathan asked Red Allen to come down to check the radio equipment and to send a message in the clear that they had captured the German station on board the ship. He also asked for permission to terminate the northern thrust of their sledge patrol unless they had further orders. Red took several minutes to study the facilities in the radio room. He was impressed with the power and fine quality of the radio. Five minutes later, he received a message from Scoresbysund.

"I have good news, Chief," Red exclaimed. "Base headquarters is certain that this station is the last operating base on the east coast of Greenland. We have permission to curtail our northerly trek and to return to base."

"That's fine, Red. Now call again in the clear asking if they can get a ski-equipped plane to transport two of our prisoners to a hospital. Tell them it's an emergency with one man in danger of a bursting appendix."

"Okay, Chief."

Nathan checked out the interior of the weather ship observing that the crew had enough food and fuel to last until spring when the ice melted and a crew could pick up the prisoners of war.

When he returned to the heated section of the ship, Red was excited about the range of the radio. "I was able to raise Coast Guard Command at Reykjavik, Iceland, over eleven hundred miles away. They have a new Grumman two engine amphibious plane with range enough to make the trip. They warned me that they would have to carefully scrutinize the weather conditions. Anticipated flying time would be eight hours one way."

"Tell them that we plan to stay at the German ship until we have word from them that the flight is underway. They can navigate with our radio signals," Nathan instructed. "In the meantime, we can scout the area for a flat landing surface.

93

Maybe we can outline the ship with a few cans of burning kerosene so that it can be seen from the air."

The sledge patrol curtailed operations. The Eskimo drivers maintained a perimeter defense out several miles of the stranded ship. They killed two polar bears to supplement their rations and those of the Germans. Nathan posted two armed guards at opposite ends of the heated living quarters on the ship. The Germans seemed resigned to their fate and offered to cook for the crew. Red Allen remained at the radio station for two days. He was able to reach Nova Scotia and Newfoundland.

On the third day of their capture of the ship, Iceland Coast Guard notified them that they had a favorable weather window of opportunity that would last for at least twenty-four hours. A flight was already enroute to pick up the two men in stretchers. They had some mail, official orders, and some fresh fruit on board. They were warned that the patients should be prepared with adequate blankets to make the trip.

The patrol team and several German soldiers helped to place barrels of kerosene along the length of the proposed runway located just a short distance from the ship on the flat sea ice. A steady vigil was placed on the bridge listening for the plane. The patients had been prepared with hot thermos bottles of tea. Their cots had been modified so that they could fit into the small cargo area of the Grumman plane. The entire German contingent eagerly assisted the patrol's efforts to make the transfer from the ship to the aircraft as quickly as possible. The plane crew needed a few minutes once they landed to fill their gasoline tanks.

Barry was the first to hear the whine of motors in the distance. Every man available lined the runway. The patients were secured to their cots and wrapped in mountains of blankets and skins. The Grumman, equipped with skis attached to its wheels, flew over the landing site making a sharp turn into the strip. They touched down, coming to a stop beside the patients. The pilot and co-pilot left the engines running and quickly began to refuel the aircraft with five gallon cans stored in the cargo area. All hands, including several German soldiers, attached the patient's cots to anchoring rings in the aircraft.

The young pilot handed Nathan a leather pouch containing mail, newspapers, and magazines, and a bag of apples. "There's also a communication from Coast Guard HQ inside, Chief. We're not going to linger. We've got a long trip back to base. Good luck."

"Thanks, Lieutenant," Nathan shook his hand and turned to the patients. "I wish you two men the best of luck. The Americans will take good care of you."

Hugo Breyman held out a hand to Nathan who grasped it. "You are a good man, Chief Collins. I will always remember your kindness."

Surprised at his expression, Nathan said, "Thank you," and tucked his hand under the blankets.

The pilot revved the plane's engines to maneuver from side to side to release the skis that had become frozen to the ice. Then he applied full power to the engines, sending the aircraft north along the ice, lifting off and making a sharp turn back to the south over the small band of men watching the plane. The sound of the engines soon became muted by the high winds, leaving each of the Coasties with a deep sense of pride that such an effort had been implemented to save the lives of two German prisoners.

Hours after the plane left, Nathan notified the patrol that they had orders to return to Scoresbysund directly. They were to leave the Germans on the ship until warm weather when a Coast Guard cutter would pick them up. The patrol was ordered to destroy every available weapon the Germans had, including the radio so that they could not send or receive messages. Nathan was ordered to assure the Germans that they would not be forgotten.

When Nathan returned to his bunk near the radio room he opened a letter from Lena:

Searsport, Maine

February 1, 1943

Dear Nathan,

I am saddened to inform you that your father died of a heart attack, two days ago. Ever since the tragedy, your mother has been bereaved to the point where she has been unable to care for Casey, so I have taken him to my apartment. He's a precious little boy who has lost his mother and now his best friend—Grandpops.

We pray that you will be able to make it home on leave soon. Your son needs to be assured that his father is alive and cares for him.

Be brave, Nathan. You are always in my prayers.

Love,

Lena

Chapter Twelve

Spring 1943

Nathan remembered how it had been in the vast frozen land in the middle of a war. Even now, nine years later, he could recall the anguish that filled his soul. Every person has important milestones in their lives. The death of his father while he was in the middle of the most difficult and dangerous mission of his life left him weakened and full of self-loathing. He had transferred the responsibility of caring for Casey to his parents when Shirley had died. Sure, he knew there was a war going on, and he could not deny that fact, but he still felt guilty.

He had always dreamed that his mother and father could lead a normal life free of responsibility when they reached retirement age. Now he was unable to do anything about the situation. He felt trapped and angry that little Casey was the victim of circumstances he could not control. His poor son… How he yearned to be with him! Lying on his cot in the hold of the German ship, tears ran into his ears. He prayed for guidance and strength from a God he did not often acknowledge as often as he should.

The sledge patrol was ordered to return to Scoresbysund by the shortest route possible for a short furlough and reassignment. They collected all of the Germans' weapons and dropped them into the waste-holding tanks and flushed the tanks by starting the main propulsion system. The Germans were literally prisoners on their own vessel. Without dogs, they could never survive an escape from the ship. Before they left the ship, Red Allen destroyed the main components to the radio, rendering it useless. The Germans had plenty of food and fuel to last until they were picked up by the Coast Guard after spring thaw.

The day after the plane left with the two sick men, the sledge patrol relinquished the safety of the ship and anxiously headed south. Their mission had been successfully completed. They had eliminated the last two German weather reporting stations in Greenland.

Two and a half weeks later, the exhausted patrol reached Scoresbysund, reporting to Hans Jessup. The farewell to their faithful Eskimos who had safely guided them through the jaws of death was an emotional experience. A bond of brotherhood had been formed that would last for a lifetime. The haggard Coastguardsmen slept for twenty-four hours straight in the warm barracks. When they awoke they drank fresh coffee and consumed large amounts of pancakes and bacon. Soon after, they were flown to Newfoundland, then to Nova Scotia, then to the Coast Guard Base at Portland, Maine. They were going home…

Now, nine years later, Nathan recalled his first furlough immediately after the Greenland patrol with distinct clarity. He had lost twenty pounds and his uniforms were a little big for him. He was anxious to see Casey and his mother who was in her early seventies. His absence from the home front when Shirley died had created a chaotic family scene. The sudden death of his father did nothing but add to the tragic situation. Caring for an energetic three-year-old boy was too much for his mother. He felt guilty that he could do little to alleviate the stressful situation.

His sister-in-law, Lena, had helped by removing some of the burden from his folks. The last letter he had received from Lena said that she was living in Searsport, a few miles north on the coast from Belfast. He had taken a bus to Belfast where he bummed a ride from an old acquaintance to his home in the outskirts of town. The house was empty. The driveway was covered with snow as if it had not been shoveled all season. He waded through it and looked for the key behind a shingle beside the door. Ah, it was still there!

Letting himself inside filled him with memories of happier times. It was cold inside. A note was on the kitchen table that the water and lights had been turned off on the fuse box in the cellar. He quickly checked the phone and to his surprise, it was still working. The operator asked for a number. She turned out to be a classmate who informed him that his mother had moved in with Lena in Searsport for the winter. She connected him to her number. The phone rang several times before his mother answered.

"Hello, Ma. This is Nathan. I'm at the old house. I have a few days leave. How are you and Casey doing?"

Mrs. Collins screamed for joy into the phone receiver. "My prayers have been answered. We've been worried about you, son. Casey has gone shopping with Lena. Lena insisted that we close down the house for the winter. Her apartment is warm and comfortable, but I'm anxious to return home to familiar surroundings."

"I have a service voucher for as much gas as I need. Could you tell Lena to come and pick me up at the house?" he asked reluctantly, uncomfortable with his predicament.

"I'll send her out as soon as she returns. How does the old house look? It was a hasty move for me. Your father's passing has torn my life apart. He was a good man, Nathan. You're a lot like him."

The emptiness of the house bought tears to his eyes. "I know, Ma... I know... Tell Lena that I'd like to get a room at the Searsport Inn."

"I'm sure she'll want you to stay here. Casey has a large room with twin beds. The two of you could sleep together. How happy he'll be to spend some time with you. He's a smart little boy. Every night he says a prayer for his dad. I'm so excited I can hardly wait to hold you in my arms again. You've been missed, my son."

"I always knew that, Ma. Tell Lena I'll be waiting. It's nice to hear your voice. I'll see you soon," Nathan said.

"I see Lena turning into the yard. She'll be there in half an hour, Nathan. Gas is scarce. Her Studebaker coupe is very good on gas."

Nathan checked the barn and the attached shed to see how much firewood was available. He found about two cords of finely split wood for the kitchen cook stove. His father had installed a kerosene heater in the parlor. Memories of happier, carefree days flashed through his mind. He wandered through each of the rooms in the house including his own on the second floor facing the road. The sun came up every morning flooding his room with bright sunshine while he lay in bed and planned each day. Frequently the moon rose out of the east splashing rays of light across his bed. As a child he had often pondered events of each day that passed and always fell asleep contented and happy with his life.

Lena honked the horn on the Studebaker coupe from the roadway, taking no chance on getting stuck in the deep snow. Nathan grabbed his duffel bag and ran across the porch to meet her.

Lena was dressed in a ski jacket with a blue kerchief over her head. She was shorter than Shirley with finely chiseled facial features giving her a more severe austere look. Her bright dark eyes were constantly taking in everything around her. She was a serious person in contrast to Shirley who was much more outgoing. Lena's no-nonsense demeanor naturally fit her career choice as a teacher. When she saw Nathan, she stepped out of the coupe to greet him. The first thing she noted about him was the deep sunken eyes and harsh lines around his mouth.

"My God, Nathan. What have they done to you?" she cried, opening her arms to him.

He accepted her embrace and held her tightly. He didn't know how to answer her question. "It's so good to be home again, Lena. I've been worried sick about Casey and Mom. Thank God you stepped up to the plate to help out."

She laid her head against his chest feeling the tenseness in his body. The concept of home for a returning warrior was filled with emotions few would ever understand. She saw the trauma in his eyes. She released him and guided him to the coupe.

"Come, Nathan. Let me take you to the apartment. We have room for you. Don't think about staying someplace else. Seeing you in uniform brings back memories of Dan Murray...

I still have dreams of him returning. This war seems to never end, and the worst is yet to come," she cried with moist eyes.

Nathan knew the cost of war. It was bad enough to see it first-hand, but the real lasting trauma was inflicted on the loved ones far away from the conflict. It was just as well that they did not know exactly how some of their loved ones died. He got into the coupe holding his duffel bag between his legs.

"Dan was a dear friend. He really loved you, Lena. He was proud that you got your teaching certificate. Over the years we shared a lot of good times together. I miss him too. Now tell me, how's Casey and Ma doing?"

Lena wiped her eyes with a handkerchief and smiled at him. "Your son is a bright ray of sunshine, Nathan. Shirley would be so proud of him. He idolized your father and prays for him, his mother and you every night."

"Words escape me, Lena. I really appreciate what you've done for Casey and Ma. I've felt guilty being away so much, placing my responsibility on everyone else."

"Please, Nathan," she pleaded, placing a comforting hand on his arm. "Don't forget that Casey is my blood nephew. Helping out where it's needed is something a family should do. After all, look at the sacrifices being made for us on the field of battle."

Nathan watched the familiar surroundings pass by as Lena turned the Studebaker towards Searsport on Route One. "It's great to be home, but somehow I feel as if I was a stranger and sort of detached from life in our small town. I expected to be more excited."

"Chief Collins, how could it be anything but different after what you've recently experienced? Give it some time. Little Casey will warm his daddy's heart, and just maybe his dad needs him more than he thinks. Well, here we are at the apartment." She pulled the coupe into a driveway and stopped.

The apartment was one of several in an old colonial building and barn on the waterfront. Lena's apartment was five rooms with a balcony facing the ocean. By the time Nathan climbed out of the Studebaker and retrieved his duffel bag, little Casey came running across the deck, throwing himself into his father's arms. He had just turned four years old and had grown much since Nathan last saw him. His mother remained on the deck with tears of relief running down her cheeks. Her only son had returned from the war! It was a time for thanksgiving.

It was an emotional reunion for everyone. His first concern was for his mother. He asked about his father's illness, and, most of all, he wanted to know how his mother was doing financially. He had the Coast Guard send two-thirds of his salary to Shirley. After her death, he continued the same to his mother. He knew that his father's retirement funds were limited. Lena had been generous enough to evaluate the situation and insist on the current living arrangements.

Casey was anxious to show his room with a view of the ocean. "Aunt Lena told me that you could sleep with me in my room." Casey said, holding his hand. Nathan noticed a photograph of him, in uniform, posted on the wall above his bed taken by his parents on their last visit to Wells. "We pray every night for you to be safe, Daddy."

It was the first time Nathan heard him use the word, "Daddy". He embraced his son and replied, "God has been good to me and answered your prayers. I've often felt the power of His presence when things looked bad. Your mother is in Heaven with Jesus. Surely she is our guardian angel that is always with both of us."

"Aunt Lena and Grandmother tell me the same things."

That evening, Nathan went upstairs to tuck Casey in bed. He kneeled beside one of the bunk beds while Casey recited his prayers. "Your prayers have helped a lot, Casey. It's nice to be here with you for a few days."

After the prayers, Casey crawled into bed, pulling one of the Hudson Bay Indian blankets up to his chin. "Are you going to stay home with us now?" Casey asked.

"I'll be with you for a few days, son. It'll give us a chance to get acquainted with each other. Goodnight, son. Pleasant dreams."

That evening, Nathan talked with his mother about local gossip and tried to plan some kind of strategy for the future. It was a time when nothing was permanent. Plans had a way of being abruptly changed by the cataclysmic events taking place across the dark waters of the Atlantic and Pacific. It was a burdensome yoke for many on the home front. Nathan was determined to help his mother to look forward with a more positive outlook. She was anxious to move back into the old house as soon as the weather warmed. Warmer days would raise her spirits, and Casey was big enough to help her around the house.

Nathan looked back on that visit with some apprehension. Lena had been most generous and helpful to his family, and he told her how much he appreciated all the assistance. She had driven him to the bus station on his last day. He could recall the conversation as they waited for the arrival of the Boston and Maine bus.

Lena had suggested that they wait in the coupe. "It really hurts to see you leave, Nathan," she exclaimed nervously.

"You've been wonderful to the family, Lena. Thanks again for everything," he had replied. "I hate to leave, too. This war will end sometime, and we can all return to a normal life."

She turned to him with moist eyes. She was on the verge of tears. "I want you to know that I'll be here waiting for you. I've always loved you, Nathan," she cried, kissing him on the lips.

He was unprepared for her demonstration of affection, returning her kiss just as the bus turned into the station. He had been searching for words and mumbled, "I'm not ready for a serious commitment just now, Lena. It's too soon… I really have to go…"

With a wave of his hand Nathan rushed to the waiting bus.

Chapter Thirteen

June and July, 1943

Nathan recalled that furlough as being one of the most difficult visits he ever had. Nothing in his life was going smoothly. He worried about his mother being able to care for Casey, and he was concerned about Lena's brash confession of love for him. It angered and upset him. The quiet ride to Boston was welcome.

He took a seat near the rear of the bus where someone had left a NY Times newspaper. He removed his cap and overcoat and placed them on the overhead luggage rack. The paper helped to bring him up to date on the progress of the war. Things were a little more positive than he realized: American forces had landed on Attu in the Aleutian Islands off Alaska: Guadalcanal had been captured in the Pacific; U.S. and British planes were bombing Germany and France on a daily basis; and the most encouraging piece of news in the paper was that large numbers of men and material were staging in the British Isles in preparation for the allied invasion of fortress Europe.

Nathan had leaned back in his seat to close his eyes. He was physically and emotionally weary. He wondered about his next duty station and really did not care what he did, but his preference was anything except for duty in the North Atlantic. Right now in the midst of the most destructive war in history, he knew that his preference had little to do with selection of duty posts. He was a faithful Coastie and would serve wherever he was needed the most.

The bus he had taken at Belfast ran to Portland where he took a Boston and Maine train to Boston. The train had originated in Bangor and was crowded mostly with men from the armed services. He placed his duffel bag on the luggage rack and sat down beside an Army sergeant sound asleep. Shortly after the train left the station, Nathan closed his eyes thinking what would happen to Casey if he was killed in the war.

Suddenly a voice from the past startled him: "Hello, Chief Collins."

He would recognize that voice anywhere! He turned to see Dr. Colleen Markey sitting across the aisle from him. She was dressed in an Army Medical Corps uniform with captain bars on her epaulettes. She was the last person in the world he expected to see. "Dr. Markey, my, what a surprise," he cried, reaching across the aisle to shake her hand.

"I thought that was you. You've lost weight, and you look drawn. Have you been wounded?" she asked. She still had that soft voice that soothed his anxieties.

"No… I just spent most of the winter in the Arctic north and haven't recuperated from the ordeal yet," he replied. "I see that you joined the Army."

The sailor sitting beside Dr. Markey offered to trade seats with Nathan so that the two could sit and visit with each other. Nathan thanked him and accepted the outside seat.

"Yes, once the war started, I felt compelled to do my share," she answered with a sober study of his appearance.

"A lot has happened since I left Wells. Congratulations, Captain. Your daughter, Cora, is a very lucky little girl. "Tell me, Dr. Markey, have you heard anything about your husband?" He turned to look at her, regretting the hurtful question.

Dark lines suddenly appeared around her eyes and mouth. She looked away from him to avoid his penetrating stare. Several silent seconds after his pointed question, she told him, "The Army has not been able to confirm or deny Donald's death or his capture. We do not know how many men have been taken prisoner or have been killed in captivity. The Red Cross have not been able to pierce the Japanese web of military secrecy. I still live with hope, but I'm enough of a realist to know that Donald's safety is a very fragile thought. His unit did surrender on Bataan. That was one of the reasons I joined the Army

Medical Corps so that I might be assigned to the Army units invading the Philippine Islands. MacArthur has promised to return. I believe that he will when that time is right."

Nathan squeezed her hand. "I'm so sorry to hear that, old friend. We live in a world tearing itself apart, but we cannot forget that it was a war not of our choosing," He wanted to change the subject and asked about her daughter. "Where is Cora? She must be talking some and almost walking by now."

Dr. Markey sighed. Her sad eyes brightened when she heard her daughter's name. "She's her mom's inspiration and reason for living. My mother and father are caring for her in the small town of Monson. I feel guilty that I can't be with her. Children need their own parents, but this war changes things…"

He saw that same positive spirit he first noticed in Wells. She was a fighter and he admired that part of her. The train had a diner car attached, and Nathan asked if he could buy her lunch for old times' sake.

She replied, "A cup of coffee would be nice."

"Does Army protocol allow an Army officer to have lunch with a Coast Guard enlisted man?" he asked, carefully making his way through the crowded train. "Wow, walking on a moving train is almost as bad as a Coast Guard cutter in the North Atlantic."

She smiled at him. "It does take a little practice. Rank does have its advantages, but friendships were formed before I put on this uniform. True friends are a rare treasure, Chief Collins."

Her words made him feel privileged to know this very special lady. He knew that he had to be careful. The bounds of friendship were carefully defined, and he was determined to not violate their sanctity.

They spent some time in the crowded diner car at the counter, sitting on stools eating sandwiches and drinking coffee. Dr. Markey asked him about his tour in the Arctic, concerned about his deep-set eyes and that stare that looked through a person without seeing them. She did not wish to press for specifics, but the experience had left a mark on him that worried her.

Nathan admitted that it was a hard tour of duty. "The Arctic is a harsh region of deadly contrasts. At times I found it fascinating and frightening all at the same time. I had discovered some things about myself that I never would have known if I had not made the journey. Peace and solitude were a part of how I recall the mission. For the first time, I experienced the fascination of complete freedom. The north's ability to punish any safety transgressions is swift and brutal. It's truly an area where the strong survive, and the weak perish." He smiled at her. "I'm probably not making much sense."

She reached and touched his hand on the counter. "You have the look of a person who has not only experienced unbridled freedom, but has danced close to the limit of what mortal man can rationally handle."

He heard the words she cautiously spoke, thinking that she had accurately described his feelings. He had also shared with her his concern for his mother and for little Casey. Not all of his trauma was inflicted by the Arctic north! He chose to keep those thoughts to himself.

"You're a keen observer of human nature, Dr. Markey. What do you say if we let someone else have our seats at the counter?" he suggested.

She shook her head in agreement and led the way back to their coach seats. She had told him that her orders were to report to San Francisco. Her flight left Boston Logan Airport early that evening. Nathan had confessed to her that he was reporting to Boston headquarters two days earlier than necessary. She had not asked him why, and he did not volunteer to inform her.

"Would it be out of line for an enlisted friend to ask an officer friend for the privilege of taking her to a club for dinner? I don't know about you, but crowds make me feel lonely."

She gave him a wistful look. "I had planned to make a short visit to Mass General Hospital where I did my internship." She hesitated and slowly asked, "Do you remember the last conversation we had when you left Wells?"

He understood her hesitation. "I remember every word... I have no intention of forcing myself upon you, Dr. Markey. The words: 'perhaps at some other time and place…' keep flashing through my mind. I admit that they were a source of comfort when solace was a scarce commodity. I withdraw my offer of dinner and apologize if I have contributed to your anxiety. I was selfishly thinking of myself. Forgive me, please."

"Forgiveness comes easy from a friend, Chief. Do not be harsh on yourself. This war has caused so much pain and sorrow. It frightens me. The killing and maiming of young men in the prime of life continues at an ever increasing rate. Sometimes I question God's reason for allowing it to continue."

Nathan took her hands in his and held them. "Be brave, dear lady. The world needs people like you more than ever. You've been a source of inspiration for me ever since we first met. As soon as we arrive in Boston you should visit the hospital. It'll be good for you. I'll help you with your luggage and to get a cab, then I'll head for Coast Guard Headquarters."

"I think that's for the best, Chief," she softly replied, avoiding his eyes.

A half hour later, the train pulled into North Station and stopped. The terminal was packed with people, mostly service men and women, coming and going. Cabs were scarce. Those in uniform were given first choice. Just outside the terminal Nathan spotted a cab discharging a fare. He ran toward it and hollered, "Are you free, cabbie? This Army doctor needs a lift to Mass General Hospital."

"You bet, Chief," the cabbie answered.

Nathan opened the door and placed her suitcase on the back floor of the cab and turned to her. "Good luck, Dr. Markey. May God be with you."

She briefly embraced him and kissed him before getting into the cab. Her eyes met his. "Goodbye, Chief Collins. You take care. I shall pray for you."

He saw tears form in her eyes as the cab left the station. He felt like running after her. Suddenly, he felt alone and insignificant. The soft-spoken doctor had left with a part of him…

Chapter Fourteen

1943-45 South Pacific Campaign

Dr. Markey had occupied Nathan's thoughts as he grabbed a cab to the Coast Guard Headquarters, Boston on the waterfront. Up to that point in the war, he believed that his experience in Greenland had to be the most dangerous undertaking of his career. Little did he know that before the war ended, he would be asked to conduct a rescue mission that was more life-threatening than the frozen north. Physical danger was a part of being a Coast Guardsman. He could take his chances like every other service man or woman fighting the war. What he was less prepared for was the emotional freight train that almost derailed him. His visit to Headquarters two days before his furlough ended set the wheels in motion for the soul-stirring crisis that tested his sanity.

His next assignment was to attend an amphibious tactical course conducted at the large Naval Base in Norfolk, Virginia. War in the Pacific necessitated the use of amphibious tactics on the multitude of small well-defended islands on the country's drive to the Japanese homeland. He was a part of the first Coast Guard detachment to attend.

The course lasted several weeks, after which Nathan was assigned to a new destroyer escort being equipped at a nearby shipbuilding facility for duty in the Pacific. He was able to get a three-day weekend pass prior to reporting to the destroyer escort. He hopped aboard a train for Belfast. Maine was already covered with ten inches of snow in mid-November. He knew that his mother and Casey had moved to the old family house in Belfast. He was anxious to see how they were prepared to handle the harsh winter months that defined his beloved state of Maine.

To his surprise, he had found that Lena had given up her apartment in Searsport and moved in with his mother and Casey. At first he thought it unusual, but when he saw how well the three got along he was pleased with the arrangement that worked well for everybody. After that visit, he did not worry as much about his mother or Casey. He had the feeling that he might not make it back home for a couple of years, so he was relieved with what he found.

He made sure they had enough firewood for a couple of seasons. The old family Chevrolet sedan was desperately in need of tires and a new battery. Auto part replacements were scarce. Most scrounged the countryside junkyards for used auto parts and tires. Lena's generous offer to use her Studebaker coupe for shopping and for any other trips within the limit of gasoline rationing rules was a great relief for Nathan.

The day he left home, he did so with a better feeling that the family was prepared for the long lonely vigil watching the war progress far from their homes. Lena graciously offered to take him to the bus station. "I leave home this time feeling better about Ma and Casey," he had told Lena. "You've made it possible, Lena. Thanks for being so generous."

She smiled, turning to him and said, "To be truthful, the situation works well for the three of us. I was finding it difficult to pay rent on my teaching salary. I love your mother. She's a wonderful person, and don't forget, I'm Casey's blood aunt. Families help each other, especially in time of war. I'm glad to do something to help."

"Your contribution as a teacher helps to keep things on the home front as close to normal as possible in time of war. It's a comfort knowing that things back home are under control. You'll never know how much your letters help. Thank you for everything."

"The last time we parted," she began hesitantly, "I was honest with you about my feelings. I later regretted it because I may have added to your anxieties for your family. I apologize for being so blunt. Having admitted that, Nathan, I hope that I'm not out of line again by asking you a question that has been on my lips for a long, long time. After this insane war is over, is there a chance that you might reciprocate with similar feelings of the heart? Please, don't answer now. Think about it, and when you've reached a conclusion, tell me honestly what your heart is telling you. The last thing I want is to send you off to war thinking that I pressured you for affections. I'm a big girl with a lot of pride, and I can handle 'no', if that is your honest choice. I'll be hoping for a 'yes', but I'll settle for a sorrowful and honest rejection."

He had sat in the little Studebaker Champion listening to her every word. He admired her honesty and integrity. In that respect, Lena had risen above the level of her dead sister, Shirley. It was a comparison that was painful for him to make, yet, it was the truth!

He took her two cold hands in his and said, "Lena, you'll be the first to know when I sort things out. Thank you for being such a wonderful, caring young lady. I can truthfully tell you that I feel privileged to call you a friend. Right now I have a lot of things running through my head. I'm not ready for a serious commitment. Too much is taking place in the world, and we cannot be assured of tomorrow as you well know." He leaned over and kissed her as the bus rolled into the station.

She returned his kiss and warmly embraced him. "I'll continue to write and to fill you on the local gossip in town. I hate goodbyes."

He grabbed his bag and rushed to the waiting bus. He had seen tears forming in her eyes as he waved and stepped onto the bus. "Nobody likes goodbyes, Lena," he mumbled to himself.

The destroyer escort he was assigned to was destined for the Pacific theatre of war after successful sea trials were completed. Nathan assisted in the placement of much of the ship's armament. The ship had twin rudders and gear-driven engine capable of propelling the sleek vessel twenty-two knots. He was impressed with its speed, maneuverability, and firepower from its nine cannons, several fifty-caliber machine gun mounts, torpedo tubes and K-gun type depth charges. It was a potent war-making machine for its small size.

The fully manned and equipped destroyer escort sailed through the Panama Canal on its way to Pearl Harbor, the last stop on American soil. It was the last time the ship could plan on sending and receiving mail direct to and from home.

Nathan had received several letters from his mother and Lena. The familiar surroundings of her home of many years was comforting to his mother. The home had memories of happier times that sustained her until her son came home from the war. She had told him how little four-year-old Casey made her proud the way he took responsibilities. The woodbox for the kitchen stove was kept full by him. His Aunt Lena and Grandmother took care of splitting kindling wood with an axe, but he promised to do that when he was bigger and stronger. That brought a smile to Nathan's lips.

The destroyer escort (DE) left Pearl Harbor escorting a convoy of freighters and troop ships destined for the Marshall Islands in the middle of the Pacific. The primary task of the DE was to protect the precious troopships within the center of the large invasion fleet. Advances against the Japanese in the Pacific Ocean area had been difficult and costly. The Japanese fought to the last man on every one of the islands. Consequently, casualties for the allies were high. Advances were made by blow torch and high explosives.

Japanese submarines were the primary threat in the central Pacific. Crews were summoned to battle stations almost on an hourly basis. The threat could be the sighting or presence of approaching enemy submarines or aircraft. The escorting ships, which included several Coast Guard cutters, then positioned themselves around the troop ships to prevent any torpedoes from touching them. The troops on board the lumbering ships understood what the fragile ships were doing and saluted their heroic efforts. By placing themselves within the line of fire, the escorts acted like bucking mustangs herding cattle.

Nathan was gunnery officer on the DE for the forward gun turrets and machine gun mounts. They were capable of shielding the troopships with a murderous rate of gunfire. The first of the Marshalls to be invaded was Kwajalen Island. It was known as Operation Flintlock. The U.S, Army's 7th Division conducted the assault across the beaches.

As the convoy approached the target, carrier planes began making heavy bombing and strafing sorties against enemy strong points prior to the landings. Experience so far indicated that the Japanese were able to resist the landing force with heavy artillery and violent machine gunfire from well-placed bunkers. It was a deadly process with heavy casualties. Once the invasion fleet was close enough for the heavy battleships and cruiser to use their large caliber artillery against the shore facilities, the troopships remained off the coast and began off-loading their infantry. The escorts continued to act as physical shields against counter-attacking Japanese submarines.

When the order from high command came to land the landing forces, the smaller cutters and DE followed the small landing craft as far ashore as their shallow-draft allowed. Nathan's ship actually ran aground on the beach so as to be close to the shore to lend cover fire for the exposed infantrymen's dash across the beaches. Gunfire erupted from countless locations on shore. Nathan directed the turret guns to select installations closest to the beach. He had three fifty-caliber machine gun mounts with orders to systematically spray the areas just inland from the sandy beaches. There was a cement pillbox directly in front of the DE. Nathan directed all weapons to concentrate on the target. Seconds later, the installation erupted with a loud explosion, clearing the way for the valiant infantry to strike further inland.

Further inland, the Japanese engaged the DE with six and eight inch cannons. It was an uneven match for the light DE whose heaviest cannon was only three inches. The tiny escort absorbed several direct hits, destroying the bridge. Nathan had taken over a 40 mm antiaircraft weapon depressed for ground support. He kept firing at the heavy weapons installation until the barrels turned cherry red. His gun tub took a direct hit from a large caliber shell. Nathan was flung high into the air falling in the water beside the crippled DE. His body almost landed on an infantryman who pulled his inert body inland to the sandy beach where he screamed to the top of his lungs, "Medic, medic…"

A young soldier with a red cross on his arm ran toward Nathan's body which was oozing blood onto the sand. His actions most likely saved Nathan's life. The medic took an M1 rifle with a bayonet attached and drove it into the sand attaching a bottle of blood plasma. A minute later, Nathan had the life-saving plasma running through his body. He was bleeding as much as he was receiving. While Nathan was being worked on by the medic in the shadow of his DE, it continued to belch fire against the shore installations.

The medic carefully lifted his body to assess his condition. He had been peppered with steel shrapnel and was bleeding profusely all over his body. The medic covered most of his wounds with sulfur powder and administered a shot of morphine to ease his pain. Nathan had a large piece of steel protruding from a gaping wound on his left side. The medic knew that his patient needed immediate surgery and left the wound for the surgeons. His final act was to note what he had done on a piece of paper, placing it in his shirt pocket. Stretcher bearers had arrived to place him in a landing craft for transport to a large hospital ship in the center of the invasion fleet offshore.

Only ten minutes had expired from the time Nathan was thrown overboard until he was placed in the landing barge enroute to the hospital ship which had available every medical care the wounded may need. Some of the men were screaming from pain, but most of them stoically suffered in silence the choppy ride out to the ship. Nathan remained unconscious while he was transferred to the hospital ship and instantly wheeled into a room where he was prepared for surgery. The attendants cut away all of his clothing and threw them in a large pile of tattered and bloody dungarees and shirts.

In this initial processing room, Nathan opened his eyes. He could remember the explosion taking place and felt himself being lifted high above the stacks of the DE. The note from the medic was taped to his naked chest while the nurses and doctors evaluated him for treatment. Stemming the loss of blood was important. Glucose and more plasma was administered while he was wheeled into the operating room. Nathan had fleeting moments of consciousness while the doctors and nurses worked on his violated body with stern faces. He felt no pain, only that he was cold.

He had suffered a broken left leg and arm. His left side required major surgery to remove the jagged piece of steel. It always amazed the surgeons how hot steel violated the young men's bodies. Several of the lacerations on all parts of his body required stitches to stop the bleeding. They took several x-rays of his body to check for internal metal shrapnel. The broken leg and arm were reset and placed in a cast. Three hours had passed before he was wheeled from the operating room to the recovery ward where he was hooked up to receive penicillin, a new antibiotic, glucose, and pain killers.

The nurses in the recovery room monitored his pulse, blood pressure, and temperature. He was running a fever, and the nurses alerted a doctor to look at him. Fate played a hand with Nathan that day. The doctor that answered a call for assistance was none other than Dr. Colleen Markey! She checked his heart and his lungs which were acceptable considering the trauma the patient had been subjected to. She ordered cold ice packs to be placed around his body and under his arms to counteract the fever caused by multiple lesions and bruises.

Dr. Markey was concerned about the patient's hearing. The blast could have burst his ear drums. She checked them and saw nothing unusual. She checked the chart on his bed and made a few notations. Names were not as important as conditions of the patients at that stage of their recovery. She had several hundred casualties to deal with, but there was something about this young man that made her feel differently. She recognized the name, Chief Nathan Collins, U. S. Coast Guard.

"My Lord, it can't be," she exclaimed aloud.

Chapter Fifteen

February, 1944

Nathan recalled that episode of his Coast Guard career with a deep respect for the generation of young men and women who had served with him. As a group they had fought two of the most militaristic nations on earth and defeated them on the field of battle. It was quite an achievement. Once the war was over, they took off their uniforms, returned to their families, and got on with their lives. Very few ever talked about their experiences in the war. It was just too traumatic to discuss with those who had not been there. It was a national generational trait that lasted for years. The horror was simply too great for family and friends to understand.

The veterans who shared the horror were banded together in a fraternity of brothers that would last their lifetime. Tears were often a part of reunions. That bond they shared with their brothers was the only source of relief for the pain. Nathan was proud to have been a part of the fraternity. He, too, had found it difficult to discuss with someone who was not there. He had seen enough bloodshed to last him a lifetime.

His presence on the huge Army hospital ship had been a transforming experience. Even now, eleven years later, he could see Dr. Markey as she administered to the wounded soldiers in her care.

Nathan remained unconscious for twenty-four hours after surgery. It was relatively dark in the ward when he opened his eyes trying to figure out where he was. The gentle rocking motion of the ship was familiar to him. The ward was quiet.

Most of the patients were asleep. He felt the pressure of the casts on his leg and arm. He had a terrible headache, and he had trouble focusing his eyes. He noted that several nurses were bent over a patient on the far side of the ward. He kept blinking his eyes and rubbing them with his right hand. A voice called to one of the nurses. He heard the voice distinctly and was relieved. He was aware that he was blown overboard, and his first worry was that he might be deaf from the explosion. His helmet had protected him from more serious injury.

One of the nurses, a young ensign, saw him move his hand across his eyes and came to his side. "Hello, Chief Collins. We've been worried about you. Do you have any pain?"

"My head aches, and I feel numb all over," he replied with a thick tongue.

"That's only normal, Chief. I'm going to have the doctor check you. Would you like something to drink? Maybe some ginger ale?"

"That would be fine, nurse."

A few minutes later, she returned with a glass of ginger ale and a straw. "The doctor will be in to see you shortly, Chief. You should drink all you can."

"Thanks."

Suddenly Dr. Markey leaned over his bed and spoke in his ear. "It's a small world, isn't it, Chief? I'm so relieved that you're awake. How do you feel?"

"I feel as if I was having a dream. Is it really you, Dr. Markey?" he focused his eyes on her.

"Yes, it's me. When I saw you it was some surprise. You're lucky to be alive, Chief. I want to check your vitals. There are cuts and bruises all over your body. We've administered glucose and antibiotics along with some blood plasma. Try to drink all the ginger ale you can. You had a very high temperature yesterday. It's normal now. You've a hardy constitution." She smiled.

How comforting it was to hear her voice. "The Irish are a tough breed," he replied with a grin. "Where am I, Doctor?"

"You're on an Army hospital ship off the coast of the Marshall Islands, Chief. I want to check your lungs and heart. I need to move you a little. Tell me if you hurt." She asked him to cough several times as she listened to his lung, and then helped him to lie flat. "Your heart and lungs are normal. You're a lucky Coastie, Chief. If you have pain I can help you."

"I really don't want to get hung up on that morphine stuff," he said. "I have good tolerance to pain. Maybe aspirin will do the trick. If not, I'll ask for something stronger." His words were slurred. He closed his eyes.

She was pleased with his response and whispered in his ear: "I agree with you, Chief. We're going to keep you here in the recovery room for a little longer. I was worried about you. You rest now and let me care for you."

The hospital ship stayed on station until Kwajalein was secured, then it moved into a deep-water cove where it could be more readily protected from submarine attack. During that week, Nathan improved a great deal. The cuts and bruises covering his body were healing to the point where they began to itch, a good sign. He still had terrible headaches that the nurses and doctors treated with aspirin. He had adamantly refused to take morphine for pain. He saw Dr. Markey almost every day. Her primary responsibilities were in the intensive care and recovery rooms.

Movies were shown every night in the wards. Nathan had watched *Gone with the Wind, Casablanca, Stagecoach,* and *Jane Eyre.* They helped build morale, and for a few moments the wounded had a chance to focus on events other than themselves. The Army medical team was first rate. Dr. Markey, with her soft voice and gentle ways, was a favorite. Nathan had a chance to watch her with the more seriously wounded men. One in particular was close to his bed. Dr. Markey had been tending to him all evening and stayed with him whispering encouragement in his ear until death mercifully interceded late that night. She slowly pulled the sheet up over his head and stood over the soldier's ravaged body silently weeping. Her ability to care touched those in the ward who witnessed her performance.

One sunny day Nathan moved his wheel chair out onto the deck. The air was fresh and sweet to smell. He had always loved the sea. This was his first time in the tropics. The entire breadth of the horizon had turned a brilliant fiery red for as far as the eye could see. It was the most beautiful sunset he had ever experienced. Its beauty had triggered a melancholic response close to tears. He had thought of home with Shirley and of Casey being alone without a dad. Memories of home were special to those so far away, but Nathan could not deny and could not control himself to not think of Dr. Markey. He had fallen in love with her from a distance, and he saw no way of changing that fact.

As if by fate, Dr. Markey stepped out on the deck looking for him. She was also touched by the beauty of the sunset before her. She saw Nathan absorbed by the spectacle, wiping his eyes, and she came to his side. "Are you all right, Chief?" she asked, noting that he turned away from her to hide his tears.

He continued to stare across the water. "I thought I was doing pretty good up to now. The sunset triggered feelings I could not control."

"Sometimes tears help flush the pain away," she replied, placing a comforting hand on his shoulder.

Nathan remained quiet for several seconds. He had to be careful and was uncomfortable not being able to control his feelings. "When will I be discharged from the ship, Dr. Markey?"

She was aware that he was changing the subject. "That's one of the reasons I wanted to speak to you tonight. An empty freighter is being equipped with beds to carry patients back to Pearl Harbor. You're one of them. A hospital will see that your bones mend properly and will give you physical therapy. Then you'll be able to return to duty."

"That will be fine. I'm feeling much better. The headaches haven't gone away, but I can live with them."

"After you leave, the hospital ship will be following the invasion force destined for the Philippines. As you know, they have a special meaning for me," she said in a low voice.

He needed to hear those words from her. They were reality and he had forgotten. He understood the anguish she so cleverly concealed. "I pray that your hopes and dreams are fulfilled. Your little daughter deserves that."

A call came over the loudspeaker paging Dr. Markey. It broke the intense emotions they both felt. "I'll see you around, Chief," she called, rushing inside to the ward.

A couple of days later, Nathan received word that he was being transferred to the large freighter coming alongside the hospital ship. He was about to be lowered into a waiting barge below when Dr. Markey rushed to see him off. "I'm glad I caught you before leaving, Chief, good luck. We always seem to be saying goodbye. I like the French way of parting: 'au revoir.' It's not as final. You take care, Coastie." she smiled and kissed him on the cheek.

He returned her smile. "Then 'au revoir' it is, Dr. Markey. Thanks for taking such good care of me. I'll never forget..."

She gave him a wistful wave of the hand as he was lowered to the barge. He looked up and returned her wave.

From that day until the war ended, his life was filled with intense activity. His therapy to regain control of his arm and leg began on the slow freighter's journey to Pearl Harbor and ended at the large Army hospital at Schofield Barracks. The base was located on a high hill, overlooking the harbor where remnants of the sunken fleet were still present lifting darkened hulls to the sky. It was a sobering reminder of why the war had to be fought.

That war against Japan was being pursued at a feverish pace even though Washington had set the policy to defeat Germany first. General MacArthur's return to the Philippines was proving to be an exercise in command that stunned the world with its precision of execution and fast pace. The controversial general had mastered the art of amphibious warfare against strong opposition. He gave textbook examples of landings that will be studied far into the future. Victories came with lower casualties than expected, a tribute to his military skills.

Nathan's stay at Schofield included a vigorous physical routine that conditioned his body. He began fulltime therapy a day after his casts were removed. Anxious to return to duty, Nathan gladly accepted the demanding schedule so as to make room for the more serious wounded men arriving daily from the battlefields. He received several letters from Lena and from his mother and Casey. The three were at his old homestead and were making out just fine. Lena had been more faithful than he expected. She did not dwell on anything negative, spending page after page on local gossip and goings-on at the small town of Belfast. Most of his male friends and classmates were in the service. A couple were killed in action, including his best friend, Don Murray. He answered the letters trying to be as positive as possible. He shared his pride with the Coast Guard effort in the war. Their footprint was much greater in the Pacific area than in the Atlantic.

The Coast Guard at Pearl Harbor had informed him that they needed experienced hands to man all of the Army ships they had assumed responsibility for during the war. By April Fool's Day, he was released from his physical therapy routines and reported for duty at Headquarters, Pearl Harbor. He was quickly attached to a new Coast Guard cutter being outfitted for duty. MacArthur was pushing the Japanese out of northwestern New Guinea and attacked Morotai Island. Nathan's new cutter followed the large fleet aimed eventually at the Philippines.

He was assigned responsibility for the forward guns on the cutter which was also equipped with torpedo tubes and depth charges. It was a job he was competent to do and drove the new crew at a hectic pace on their long journey to Morotai Island. The cutters were of shallower draft than most of the Navy ships except for the fast and nimble plywood PT boats. The cutters could get in close to the beaches with gunfire support for the infantrymen storming ashore. They were capable of destroying enemy strongholds up to a half mile inland. The two three inch cannons on the cutter belched destruction to the Japanese during the initial landings. The quad-fifty-caliber machine gun mounts were vicious support weapons with a withering rate of fire pulverizing anything within their range. Their performance was greatly admired by the advancing infantrymen.

The Coast Guard cutters performed well working within Admiral Halsey's third Fleet. This was MacArthur's navy element and he was relentless in his drive for speed and performance toward the Philippines. Nathan and his shipmates were pleased to be a part of the first team striking a blow for victory, even though they were driven to the limits of their endurance.

Once Morotai was neutralized, plans were underway to attack Mindanao to the north. It was to be the first step to the Philippine Islands. Carefully prepared plans were abruptly laid to one side when Admiral Halsey informed MacArthur that he was experiencing relatively light resistance to his advances into the South Pacific area. Therefore, an assault on Leyte was substituted for mid- October.

Nathan remembered that event with mixed emotions. He never forgot how things came about in such a manner that fate seemed to dictate the course of events. Just to think about that time and place sent chills up his spine.

Preparations for the assault of Leyte were concentrated on the eastern coast of the island on Leyte Gulf. The Western shoreline was less populated and less accessible by ocean going vessels. Countless small islands dotted the western coastal area. It was in this area of relatively shallow water channels that the Coast Guard was well suited and equipped with their shallow draft ships to perform well. The new cutter entered the sea between Leyte and Cebu to the west where they destroyed several small Japanese barges and supply vessels with wooden hulls. PT boats worked with them in this type of marine environment.

The date set for the assault on Leyte was set for October 20, 1944. On October 10th, the Coast Guard cutter received the following urgent message in code:

SECRET:

FROM: Sixth Army Headquarters, Hollandia, New Guinea

TO: Lieutenant Matthew Rogers, Captain, U.S. Coast Guard, Cutter 965

SUBJECT: Immediate rescue of American POW inmates on Leyte

As you already know we will be invading the island of Leyte soon. We have already executed several behind the lines rescue of American POWs prior to the invasion with the express purpose of preventing the Japanese from murdering the inmates to hide their trail of torture and death.

One such operation known as Operation *Dragonfly* has been cancelled because of an accident on the submarine carrying a contingent of Army Rangers. You are requested to acknowledge immediately if you can provide a nine-man landing force to execute this mission prior to the main invasion. An affirmative from you will be followed immediately by the information giving time and place needed to successfully carry out the mission.

Time is of the essence.

Lieutenant General Walter Kreuger
Commanding General Sixth Army

Chapter Sixteen

Operation *Dragonfly*, October, 1944

Captain Rogers called Nathan into the officer's mess on the cutter. "Chief, I've just received a request we can't gracefully refuse. Sixth Army has asked us to provide a nine-man landing force to conduct a rescue operation of American POWs stationed on Leyte. We have no particulars beyond what I've just told you. What do you think?"

"Why can't the Army Rangers do it?" he asked, interested in the operation.

"This operation has already been planned. Rangers have been sidelined on a submarine that cannot make the deadline. If I said 'yes' would you take charge of the landing party?"

Nathan knew the hot potato would be given to him. "Sure, I'll take the job, Captain. I want to personally pick the men though. The Coast Guard always stands ready to rescue those in need."

Captain Rogers breathed a sigh of relief. "I had a feeling you would be the right man for the job. Take your pick of the men, and I'll answer General Kreuger's message. You may have to travel light and fast. We have enough Thompson submachine guns in the armory room for your squad. Semper Paratus, Chief."

"Semper Paratus, Captain. I'm about to shrink your gunners on the ship," Nathan replied with a grin.

An hour later, the cutter received confirmation orders for Operation *Dragonfly*. Nathan and his nine-man task force were scheduled to be picked up by a PT boat which would insert them on an isolated coconut plantation on the west coast of

Leyte. They were waiting in the enlisted men's mess room fully equipped with ammunition, water canteens, first aid kits, and several extra field c-rations when a sleek and deadly PT boat suddenly arrived on their port side to pick them up.

The PT boat commander was a young ensign with light blond hair. He warmly welcomed the Coast Guardsmen aboard his craft, offering them to gather around in the bridge. He had just been assigned to the operation after news of the submarine mishap with instructions to lie off a particular point of land until dusk when he would be able to make contact with a band of Filipino partisans. He told Nathan that he was not going to risk beaching his boat and that he would insert the team ashore by inflated rafts.

Nathan carried a small signal lamp with him to signal the PT boat when they returned to the coast to be picked up. At the time, Nathan wondered how many inmates they would find in the prison compound. The Ensign did not have any more information than Nathan was given by his Captain. He was informed that the partisan group carried a portable radio with them, and they could answer all of his questions once they made contact.

They traveled north at a rapid speed until the sun began to set. Ensign Howe ordered the craft to a slow crawl, pointing off to their starboard to what looked like a palm tree plantation with the trees planted in straight rows. It was getting dark, and soon the individual trees could not be distinguished. Ensign Howe gave orders to shut down the engines. A small point of light blinked three times and was repeated a few seconds later. It was the signal from the partisans to land the Americans.

Nathan instructed each of his men to check and load their pistols and Thompsons, being sure to keep them on safety with a round in the chamber. They had to be prepared for the unthinkable, which he knew from experience was always a possibility. Inflatable rafts were placed in the water to transport the men to shore. He gave a crisp salute to Ensign Howe as he stepped into the raft.

"Good luck, Chief. We'll be here off shore and on station every evening at about this time until you return. The Navy salutes our Coast Guard brothers."

The trip ashore seemed an eternity. Sitting in the crowded raft made him uncomfortable. What were they going to find ashore? The minute the rafts touched the beach the Coasties scrambled inland, taking cover in the low growing vegetation between the beach sand and the coconut grove, throwing themselves on the ground in a defensive semi-circle alert for anything that moved. For fifteen minutes they lay and listened. The muffled rumble of the powerful Packard engines of the PT boat could be heard as Ensign Howe slowly drew further away from the shore.

Suddenly a voice from the dark interior of the plantation muttered two words: "Operation *Dragonfly*."

Still uncertain if he had entered a trap, Nathan nervously answered, "Operation *Dragonfly*."

Upon hearing an American voice, a Filipino patriot approached the Americans. "We've been expecting you. Which one of you is Chief Petty Officer Collins?"

Nathan breathed easier and stood up. "I'm Collins. You've probably been notified about our substitution for the Army Rangers. The Coast Guard is proud to volunteer for this worthy mission. How far away is the prison stockade?"

"It's about ten miles inland, Chief. Soon the moon will be out, and we can travel with ease. I'm Lieutenant Malcolm, commander of a platoon of Filipino Army partisans. We will assist you in attacking and killing the Japanese who run the camp."

"Do you have your platoon here with you in the plantation?" Nathan asked, straining to see in the semi-darkness.

"Oh, yes. They've circled the plantation so you do not have to worry about being discovered by the Japanese," Lieutenant Malcolm replied.

"How many Japanese guard the camp?"

"The camp operates a small copper mining operation. The inmates dig copper ore, cuprites. The ore is then hauled to a smelting plant near a railhead that runs to the east coast on Leyte Gulf. The size of the prisoner work force has been drastically reduced by disease and starvation. There are approximately twenty to thirty Americans left now. The

Japanese have about twenty men in their garrison force. Most are Japanese naval infantry, the most vicious Japanese soldiers we have encountered. We have studied the routines of the compound and arrived at a plan of attack. If you don't mind, we can discuss it in detail when we arrive at an excellent overview of the surrounding area. The moon is high enough for us to travel now, Chief."

"I understand, Sir. I'm pleased to rely on your expertise, Lieutenant. We'll follow in single file behind you, assuming that your men will secure the flanks and the point of our column," Nathan suggested to this sturdy Filipino patriot.

The Coast Guard task force walked behind Nathan and Lieutenant Malcolm alert and prepared for any emergency even though their flanks were protected. Halfway to the camp, Lieutenant Thompson signaled that they stop for a rest and for them to be silent.

"This will be a good time for you and me to discuss tactics we should use when we arrive at the camp, Chief Collins," the intrepid patriot suggested, laying a small map on the ground in front of Nathan. "I have a blanket to place over our heads so that we can use my flashlight to study the map. One can never be too cautious."

"I agree, Lieutenant. I'm anxious to see what you have in mind," Nathan replied enthusiastically. He saw the hand drawn sketch outlining their line of approach to the prison camp and to the open-pit mining operation. The layout of the prison compound was a simple square configuration with the prisoner's huts just inside the barbed wire fence south of the Japanese barracks. Sturdy elevated guard posts were built into each of the four corners of the fence.

"There is a small wooden structure used as an infirmary in the southwest corner of the compound away from the stinking open slit trenches that permeate the area," Lieutenant Malcolm pointed on the sketch. "The POWs sleep in three-sided grass and bamboo huts. The overview we are headed for is located on a hill immediately north of the barracks building and south of the large open-pit mine with a good view of the entire compound. My men will surround the compound and attack all four corners at the same time. We are adequately equipped to handle this operation, Chief."

"That sounds like a good tactic, Lieutenant," Nathan commented.

"While we are securing the general vicinity of the prison, you and your men can storm the front gate located here on the east side of the fence. You should then rush to surround the grass huts the prisoners sleep in to protect them from any last minute attempts by the Japs to massacre the men."

"What about the barracks?" Nathan asked.

"The barracks will be destroyed by my men in coordination with the guard tower assaults. We will attack swiftly with deadly force to completely throw the Japs off guard. Speed is important as we have found from experience," Lieutenant Malcolm replied. "You should also know that another partisan group is going to occupy the rail head from the mining operations so that no Japanese reinforcements can reach the compound."

"I detect a certain professionalism in your tactics, Lieutenant Malcolm, and your English is flawless. Where did you pick that up?" Nathan asked curiously.

The Filipino smiled. "I was selected a few years ago by General MacArthur, along with several others, to study infantry tactics at your famous U.S. Army's Fort Benning Infantry School. I was in the United States for over a year. I was commander of a platoon of Filipino Scouts when the Japs invaded my country."

"It's a privilege to serve with you, Sir," Nathan told him. He and his Coasties were in good hands!

The column continued its trek towards the prison camp. Nathan suggested that his men open some of their field rations and take some nourishment. Nathan had a fondness for the chocolate in the rations. He was pleased to know that Filipino forces were taking care of any external threat while his Coasties broke through the gate, eliminating any Japanese elements within the compound. He was anxious to learn about the condition of the prisoners. Lieutenant Malcolm had warned him that they would probably find that most of the inmates would be grossly undernourished and in poor physical condition, with many individuals near death from starvation. They arrived at the overview while it was still dark. The men took positions behind shrubbery and anxiously waited for the coming dawn.

Lieutenant Malcolm had a radio man with him and was busy relaying instructions for his men to execute the tactics he had previously set up with them. He was unconcerned if the Japanese were trying to locate his radio signal. The days of Japanese occupation of his country were numbered and were about to change. The patriotic Filipinos were prepared to rise up and strike a blow for freedom in conjunction with their American benefactors.

Nathan laid out a scheme of maneuver with his nine men. They would force the main gate immediately after the four corner guard posts were blown. Once inside the wire compound, Nathan would lead the men north between the barracks and the grass huts to place a ring of security around the inmates. He instructed the men to holler to the prisoners that they were Americans and for them to remain low in their shelters until they had secured the compound. "Be sure to tell the men that they are free and that we are Americans."

The sun filled the eastern horizon with a brilliant red-orange hue prior to rising above the distant mountains. Now Nathan could see the compound and studied the flimsy shelters used by the American soldiers. Lieutenant Malcolm pointed to the main gate and waved to him. He was joining the group attacking the Japanese barracks. He had pointed for Nathan to carefully crawl towards the main gate through the tall grass surrounding the area. Nathan and his men succeeded in reaching a good location to launch their attack.

The stillness of the early morning erupted in a crescendo of violence and explosions as the guard posts and the main gate were blown to pieces by hand grenades. Their surprise had been complete. Nathan ran through the demolished gate firing his Thompson from the hip at two Japanese soldiers inside the gate. He and all of his men were inside the compound before all of the pieces settled to the ground. His force split into two groups as planned with every man screaming for the Americans to remain inside their huts out of the line of fire. Just as his team cleared the northern corridor around the huts they ran into a squad of Japanese soldiers who had probably been posting sentries.

The speed of the attack against the compound worked to the advantage of the Filipinos and the Coasties who stopped and drew a firing line against the Japanese with all guns spraying the area. Nathan was grazed on the neck with a bullet. He was unaware of it until his neck and shoulder felt wet. Continuing to ignore the wound, Nathan directed fire against the Japanese within the compound, snapping a fresh ammunition clip onto his Thompson. He could hear heavy gunfire all around the perimeter. Grenades and mortars could be distinguished from the crisp snap of small arms fire.

As soon as the four guard platforms were eliminated, Lieutenant Malcolm had ordered his men to close immediately to place a ring of security around the living area of the American prisoners. The Japanese barracks north of the fence suddenly exploded into a large puff of black smoke. A rousing cheer came from the American prisoners as the debris settled to the ground.

At that point, Nathan instantly ordered his men to turn out the American soldiers so that he could get an accurate count and an assessment of the men's condition. He slung his Thompson over his shoulder and entered the nearest grass hut.

"Do not be afraid. I'm an American and we have come to set you free. The Japanese cannot harm you anymore. We have come to take you home," Nathan said, adjusting to the dim light of the windowless structures. "Would those of you who can, please step outside of the hut? Do not be afraid. I'm an American Coast Guardsman. Please... do not be afraid. Come out so that we can take a count of how many Americans are in the camp. I understand that our sudden appearance is a shock to all of you, but we need to know how many are here. Please... do not be afraid."

Very slowly, ghost-like figures began to file out of the grass huts into the morning sun. Nathan never forgot that first glimpse of the American soldiers in the camp. One tall emaciated man with the look of death in his deeply sunken eyes, faced Nathan with an expression of disbelief and horror.

Tears welled into his eyes and ran down over his grimy cheeks. Nathan's heart went out to the man, embracing him, as the other walking skeletons exited the hut. Some had emotionally and psychologically retreated to a world they may never be able to leave. Partial blindness was rampant throughout the camp, caused by their starvation diet. Loss of teeth and hair was common.

Nathan released the man in tattered clothing. "We have come to free you Americans. Can anyone tell me who the senior officer among you?"

The man Nathan had embraced straightened his back, standing up straight to answer, "I'm the ranking officer. I'm Captain Hank Jones. We prayed for help, but none came. In time we all simply gave up. Many of our comrades have laid down and willed themselves to die so as to be free of pain and suffering. In many ways they were the lucky ones. I was captured on Bataan with my infantry company. I'm partially blind, so tell me what has taken place here?" Captain Hank Jones asked in a weak voice. "Have the beasts really been killed?"

"That is true, Captain Jones," Nathan explained to the group before him. "I am a Coast Guard chief petty officer, and I salute you and your men, Sir. We have been joined by many brave Filipino patriots who have secured the outer perimeter of the prison and mine complex. The Japanese have either been killed or have left the area. You are free. We have here with us the commander of the Filipino troops."

Lieutenant Malcolm acknowledged the men before him. "I apologize for not coming to your aid sooner, but it was impossible. Rejoice now that the powerful American Army and Navy are about to liberate the Philippines. You are among the first to be freed."

Nathan anxiously turned to Lieutenant Malcolm, "Will you get whomever it is that you report to on the radio? I don't care if you have to call General Krueger's Sixth Army Headquarters, we've got to get food and medical supplies to these men. They'll never be able to walk out of this jungle! We need it now, not later..."

"Settle down, Chief," Lieutenant Malcolm said, placing a hand on his shoulder. "I've already called in for an air drop of food, medicine, and clothing for the inmates. They promised prompt delivery and security of our outer flanks by Naval air power operating from carriers already in Leyte Gulf."

Nathan smiled at his companion. "You've exceeded my expectations, Lieutenant Malcolm. Thank you for being so efficient."

"Don't forget, Chief. This is my country, and I love it as much as you do yours. By the way, when my men threw a protective ring around the compound, they discovered a few sick soldiers in a wooden building used as an infirmary just inside the fence. It was being run by an American doctor. I advised him of the situation, and suggested that he get ready to accept more patients if he had room. When the air drop comes, he'll have more supplies to dispense. Aside from hunger, these men need treatment for malaria more than any other disease."

The overpowering of the compound went better than Nathan expected. His most pressing immediate problem was to get some food, anything they could scrounge, into these starving American soldiers. He ordered two of his men to check if any facilities were usable at the Japanese barracks; if not, try to locate where they stockpiled food for the garrison troops. He ordered them to collect all of the C-rations available among the Coasties and to distribute them as fairly as possible with the help of Captain Jones. It was a start!

Captain Jones told him, "I'll do as you request, Chief. I should also tell you that the men voted me their commanding officer. There is a senior Army officer in the infirmary."

The Filipino troops had established a security ring around the compound so that they could care for the soldiers. In the distance they heard loud explosions to the east where MacArthur's air force was eliminating Japanese strongholds prior to the invasion.

Without warning, two sleek silver P-38 fighters flew over the compound a few feet above their heads. The craft wagged their wings to acknowledge the freed prisoners. Then they peeled off to the left and to the right clearing a path for two DC-3 transport planes to drop supplies by parachutes onto the compound. It made Nathan proud to be an American. The inmates watched the white chutes float to the ground with tears in their eyes. The presence of airplanes over their compound erased any doubt they may have had that they were truly free. The United States of America had not forgotten them! MacArthur's promise to return was evident.

"Lieutenant, tell the airmen of our situation and that we will have to figure some way of getting these men out of the jungle to the coast. Walking out is not an option. Tell them thanks for the drop. They have saved the lives of most of the men in our care."

Filipinos and Coasties were scrambling to collect and concentrate the supplies dropped by the two transports. Within an hour they had a gas-fired field kitchen operating full blast turning out bread and heating water for coffee or tea. The men were preparing a meal of rice and chicken for immediate consumption. It was nourishing and compatible so that their shrunken stomachs could digest the food. The aroma of baking bread from the field kitchen wafted across the compound to the silent prisoners. It was an aroma that brought back fond memories of better days and happier times. The scent of food raised morale of the inmates a good thirty percent.

Captain Jones asked the men from different huts to select those men in need of immediate medical attention. Stretchers had been dropped for their use.

Les Perkins, a tall lanky farmer from South Dakota who had been designated by Nathan as second in command, carried a large box of assorted medical supplies to the wooden infirmary at the far end of the compound. Ten minutes later Les came running back to Nathan.

"Chief, you're not going to believe it. The infirmary is as bad as the grass huts here. There are four men inside and a few more pallets available. The men are in dire shape or dead, Chief. You've got to see it to believe it..."

"What's wrong, Les?" Nathan asked impatiently.

"The doctor in there is unable to stand on his two feet. He's dead drunk..."

Chapter Seventeen

Operation Dragonfly, October 1944

"You mean drunk?" asked Nathan.

"That's for sure. I saw an empty bottle of sake on the table, Chief."

"Well, we can't do anything about that right now, Les. The men are beginning to get some food into their stomachs. My god, what a horrible time these men must have had. Do you have any suggestions about getting them to the coast, Les?"

"My guess is that we have about twenty-five men to be concerned about. There was an abandoned trailer near the infirmary. Maybe we could use it to carry some of the weakest men," Les offered with a hunch of his shoulders.

"I think you may be on to something, Les. There are a few mules at the pit site. We'd need a minimum of four to five carts. Getting them through the jungle won't be easy, but we can do it," Nathan remarked.

His conversation with Les formulated a plan to evacuate the camp. The soldiers would have to use their old huts for one more night. He asked Les to bring the sick soldiers and the inebriated doctor to the grass huts so that they were all together and could be protected easier. "Bring any supplies you may find in the infirmary, Les. If the doctor can't walk, carry him to one of the huts and deposit him with the rest of the men."

By nightfall, Nathan was satisfied with the way things had turned out. Lieutenant Malcolm's men had located five mules and harnesses to pull wagons for the soldiers' evacuation from the camp. Both men agreed that it was important for the men to get to medical treatment as soon as possible. The inmates followed Captain Jones's orders without question. The pride of being a soldier again was beginning to show in the men. It was a tribute to the leadership qualities of Captain Jones, a West Point graduate who lived up to the high expectations of his alma mater.

The field kitchens were being run at capacity by two Coasties turning out bread loaves, massive amounts of rice, chicken soup, and string beans. They were attempting to prepare enough for the soldiers until they were deposited on the ships waiting for them.

Nathan posted two Coast Guard pickets within the compound prepared to be rotated at midnight. He intended to take one of the picket slots at that time. Once the camp had settled down to sleep, he stretched out on the cool, moist ground. It felt good to his sweat-stained body. The humid, oppressive air of the tropics was in stark contrast to his tour in the arctic north.

Lieutenant Malcolm sat beside him. "I'm going to turn in, too, Chief. I want to share a few things with you. I've just been ordered to carry out a mission to destroy a couple of bridges prior to the landing in a few days."

"That complicates our movement through the jungle with the cart caravan," Nathan frowned. "We might need three days having to clear a passageway for the carts."

"Your mission of transporting the prisoners to the coast has priority, Chief Collins. If I left a driver with each cart for you and two or three for convoy escort, would you feel comfortable? I know it's asking a lot for your men, but I've been given strict orders. You know what that means," the Lieutenant shook his head.

"Orders are meant to be carried out, Lieutenant. What are our chances of running into a Japanese patrol?"

"Fifty, fifty with the alerting of the whole Japanese Army on Leyte, Chief. They probably will not pursue your convoy, but they may have stepped up recon patrols believing an invasion imminent. My partisans have to face the same possibilities."

"You and your patriots have done a wonderful job of making Operation *Dragonfly* a success. I'm thankful for that.

Tomorrow morning we'll take our chances and make a dash for the coast," Nathan smiled. "Hell, Coasties are used to doing with less. It's a way of life with us! Thanks for everything, Lieutenant."

The next morning, cooks on the field kitchen provided a large serving of scrambled powdered eggs and hot oatmeal for all of the soldiers. They ate ravenously until they could hold no more. Nathan saw a marked improvement among the walking inmates. Each cart contained five men. Nathan wanted to maintain as much as possible the feeling of community among the soldiers. Quinine for malaria was administered to all of the soldiers. The air drop of supplies had been sufficient to give every man a tan shirt, a pair of pants and Army shoes. Their transformation from prisoners to soldiers was an inspiring experience for Nathan and his Coast Guard contingent.

The convoy of five carts each pulled by a single mule guided by one of the Filipino partisans got underway as soon as the soldiers were fed their morning meal. Nathan said goodbye to Lieutenant Malcolm, and paired Les with the guide who knew the direction to the coast, acting as point for the convoy. Nathan and his remaining Coasties walked beside the carts ever alert for an enemy ambush. They removed small trees and anything that would hinder their passage along the trail the guide had selected. It was hard work in the heat and humidity of the rain forest, but everyone was encouraged that they were underway.

The soldiers had said goodbye to their prison compound by burning the grass huts and all of the excess supplies dropped by the planes. Some of the soldiers curiously asked about the progress of the war. They had not heard anything since they were captured in 1942. No mail, no Red Cross packages, and no medicine for their duration. They had walked daily to the open pits to shovel bauxite ore into the very carts being used to carry them to freedom. Nathan saw poetic justice in that act.

Several soldiers told Nathan that, about a month ago, they had been the recipients of hundreds of small boxes containing candy, cigarettes, paper and pencil and sewing supplies. They were dropped by two low-flying transport planes. One had kept a box and showed it to Nathan. It was covered with

American and Philippine flags with the message, "I shall return." printed on the two sides. They were known as victory packages and originated at MacArthur's Headquarters. These small boxes rejuvenated the men's hope and dreams for the future. The only down side to their presence was that the Japanese were even more brutal than ever. The threat of death at the hands of the ignorant guards was a distinct possibility. They were barely fed enough to stay alive to shovel bauxite ore.

The first day of travel was uneventful. A good sign! That first night, Nathan sat down against a palm tree to rest until it was his turn at the outposts. Captain Jones had joined him, finding it awkward to balance himself down into a sitting position. "Where are you from, Captain Jones?" Nathan casually asked.

"I was born and raised in Iowa where my father raised soy beans. I knew early in life that farming was just not for me, so I took a test for West Point and was accepted. I've never regretted it. It was our luck of the draw to be hung out to dry at Bataan. Half of the men in the camp were captured there."

"I just checked the men in the carts. They're accepting this ride to our pickup point as if it was a lark."

"How could it be any different, Chief? If you've never experienced excessive brutal treatment, you can never appreciate what it was like at the camp or know what the loss of freedom can do to the human soul. You and the wonderful Filipino partisans have killed those who brutalized us. It was an act of justice well administered. This is the first time in almost three long years that we could even think about freedom. I expect that we'll be in therapy for a long time to overcome what it was like back there. You can see already what a few good meals and clean set of clothes do for the human spirit. I'm so proud of these men."

Nathan had caught a glimpse of what made this walking skeleton officer sitting beside him a leader of men. Respect for the men came from the top down instead of from the bottom up.

"I've been concerned about the doctor we found at the infirmary. The building was almost empty and had very little medical equipment. When we arrived he was drunk and had passed out on Japanese sake. I just saw him hunkered down in one of the carts. He seemed to be in another world. I would never try to judge any man who had to endure what you've been through, but my instincts tell me that a doctor should be more concerned about his patients. The men in his hut helped him into the waiting cart this morning. What happened to him, Captain?"

"Contrary to the noble standards of society, every man has his breaking point, Chief Collins. Some have greater tolerance to abusive tactics, be they physical or mental. Both are capable of crippling a human being. I'll leave that judgment to God. The Major was on Bataan with us. I never served with him, but he was part of the Army that surrendered to the Japanese. Somehow he was able to get enough medicinal alcohol to become addicted to the stuff. Maybe it was something else, I don't know, and I never tried to find out."

"Did he get special treatment from the Japanese?" Nathan asked, knowing that Captain Jones was reluctant to answer his questions.

"You ask what cannot be known for certain. I will tell you that I tried to get him to take responsibility for the camp. His rank as major was the most senior of our group. He adamantly refused the position. I never asked him why, and that's all I'll say about the man. End of conversation, Chief," Captain Jones stated with conviction.

Nathan understood. "You're a good officer, Captain Jones. I've served under men like you. I'm sorry to have pried into something that's none of my business. It's time for me to relieve one of my men. Goodnight, Captain."

"Goodnight, Chief Collins. We're so thankful that you came for us. A few more days of captivity would have drastically dwindled our ranks. The men were at that point where release from the torment was eagerly sought. I know that I was seeking that freedom from pain and misery. In the years to come, you'll have quite a story to share with your grandchildren."

Nathan watched the proud professional soldier walk away, and turned to dress the small wound he had received on his neck. He treated it with sulfur powder before wrapping his neck with a clean bandage and replaced his shirt.

The next morning, the caravan was put into motion a half hour after sunrise. They came to a stream shortly after leaving the compound. Two of the wagons had already crossed the stream without incident when gunfire ripped through the silence of the tropical forest. Les and the Filipino guide ran back to the column hollering for everyone to lie low in the wagons and for the drivers to bunch the wagons close together. They had been jumped by a Japanese patrol of maybe eight to ten man.

After the initial burst of gunfire, the Japanese quit firing. The column waited for several minutes in silence. The Japanese had broken their patrol into two groups that hit them on both flanks at the same time. Nathan had split his own forces in half expecting the rush to their vulnerable flanks. The screaming enemy soldiers hit them with a volley of fire that helped expose their own positions. Nathan's task force was equipped with Thompsons which put out a withering shield of lead against the enemy lines. They followed up with a rush toward the Japanese flinging hand grenades every step of their advance. The fanatical attackers were silenced.

Nathan called for a report on casualties. One mule was killed and three soldiers in the first cart were wounded. Nathan offered Captain Jones his first aid kit to care for the wounded and went to get the doctor. He yelled for the Major to help out at the first cart. There was no reply. Nathan ran to the cart where he had last seen the doctor, finding him sitting up holding onto his head with both hands. "Major, we have some wounded men who need you. Do you hear me?"

One of the soldiers lying on the floor of the wagon spoke up. "He was sleeping almost as if he had been drugged."

Nathan shook him by the shoulder. "Can you help us with the wounded men?" It was more a desperate demand than a request.

The Major looked up at him, shaking his head as if to say "no." Nathan could not see anything wrong with the man. As a matter of a fact, he had considerably more weight on his bones than any of the other inmates.

Nathan asked again in a loud voice. "Are you going to help your fellow soldiers?"

Again, a nod of the head.

Infuriated beyond control, Nathan picked up the man, holding him like a baby and threw him into the river they were trying to cross. "Now maybe you can answer some of my questions. Are you or are you not a doctor?"

The sudden dunking in the cool water revived the Major enough that he accepted Nathan's hand to climb out of the mountain stream to the shore. "Yes, I'll look at the soldiers," he said in an unsteady voice.

"They're in the first wagon," Nathan pointed. "Can you walk?" It was a spiteful question the Major refused to answer, using the wagons and mules to steady his progress to the wagon at the head of the column.

One of the soldiers had already died. Their weakened condition gave no reserve to fight the trauma of bullet wounds. Two Coasties carried the dead man and deposited him in the last wagon. They told Nathan that the dead man deserved a military burial once they were on board a ship.

The incident about the Major not only angered Nathan with the man, he was disappointed with himself that he had lost control in front of the other men. The doctor did not mix well with the soldiers. They tolerated him, but did not accept him as one of their own. There was a strange silence about who he was and what he had done during their incarceration at the camp. According to Captain Jones, he never worked as a laborer in the mines.

Curious about his role as a physician, Nathan checked on what was taking place in the first wagon. Les and Jones were standing by in case they were needed. The Major had asked the wounded where they were hit. One had a bullet shatter his left arm. The other man had a superficial wound on the calf of his right leg.

The Major looked up to see Nathan staring at him and said, "This man is going to lose his arm. I cannot surgically remove it now. If I wrap it tightly with compression bandages, they should hold it until we have better facilities. The other man will be alright if we keep the wound from getting infected."

"Thank you, Doctor."

"Captain Jones and the Coast Guardsmen have done a good job of stemming the excessive bleeding on the wounded men. I have covered the wounds with sulfur powder. The bandages should be changed twice daily here in the tropics. I see that we now have the luxury of sufficient medical supplies. That was not always the case," the Doctor replied with a penetrating stare into Nathan's thoughts.

"You may ride in this wagon or you may return to your original location. If I prejudged you and stepped out of line, I apologize. I was hoping we could make it to the coast without casualties. When I saw the three soldiers hit, I felt responsible. I took their injuries personally," Nathan told him.

"I'll stay with the wounded in the wagon. You are not the only one to have experienced despair, Chief Collins."

"Let's get this convoy moving again. We've got a date with the U.S. Navy, and we don't want to be late," Nathan cried out loud. One wagon was left behind with the dead mule.

The lumbering wagons made slow but steady progress through the jungle without a cleared roadway. He went ahead with the Filipino scout and Les to pick a suitable site to spend the night. They carried enough drinking water for themselves, but the mules needed water also. Late in the afternoon when long shadows were cast on the tropical forest floor, they found an ideal location to stop and rest for the night. Nathan directed that the wagons park close to each other for protection and in case of rain so that tarps could be placed over the soldiers.

That evening, while everyone was eating something from their C-rations, Captain Jones told him that the lead scout estimated that they could make it to the coast the next day. They were about halfway there now. That was encouraging news. He sat down against one of the wagon wheels and munched on a candy bar. He was more tired from the heat and humidity than from the physical exertion.

The rest of the trip to freedom went as smoothly as anyone could ask for. The exhausted column entered the open spaces of the coconut plantation just as the sun disappeared in the west. The dark shadows under the canopies had an ominous air to them. It made them feel vulnerable and readily visible from the sea or land. Discovery by a curious water or land patrol was possible. Therefore, Nathan called all of the Coasties and Filipinos together to lift the soldiers from the wagons and place them in a secluded area close to the open sand beaches. He then bid farewell to the faithful Filipino patriots who removed the mules and wagons from the vicinity of the plantation.

Using the small signal lamp from his pack, Nathan blinked three short light signals against the blackness beyond the pounding waves. His heart pounded when three distinct blinks were directed from offshore to them on the beach. He waited a few minutes and repeated the signal. It was answered one more time.

He was elated. "All we've got to do now is wait for them to come to us, Les."

"I'll feel better when all of these men are safe on board, Chief."

A half hour later, they saw several rubber rafts and motorized boats climb up on the sand. They were from the Coast Guard Cutter *Northland*. Quietly and efficiently the entire group of Coasties and soldier inmates were whisked off the beach and brought to the cutter. They were once again on American property!

The PT boat originally assigned to Operation *Dragonfly* had run aground on unchartered reefs. Therefore, the nearest Coast Guard cutter was assigned the job of extracting the column. Captain Rogers was prepared to receive the former prisoners and care for their needs. He asked for and received several pharmacist's rates from a larger Navy vessel.

Once on board the *Northland* the soldiers were given thorough physical examinations, a short haircut, sprayed with DDT to decontaminate them from the vermin they carried on their bodies, and, finally, were assisted to warm showers. After that, they were given a clean set of clothes and treated to a hot meal of coffee, chicken, mash potatoes, peas, topped off with apple pie and ice cream.

By the time they had completed all of the preliminary functions the men were exhausted. The Coasties set up mattresses, blankets and pillows wherever they could find space. The men were quick to settle down for the evening.

Nathan and Captain Rogers retired to the officers' wardroom to enjoy another cup of coffee. They were soon joined by an anxious Captain Jones.

"Excuse me, Chief. I'm missing one man from our POW list!"

Nathan looked at Captain Rogers, "Were any of the men taken to different locations on the ship, Sir?"

"Not that I know of, but I'll find out," Captain Rogers responded, leaving the wardroom. He called to the bridge and ordered a top to bottom search of the ship for one of the missing soldiers.

While the search was taking place, a Coastie entered the wardroom with a set of dog tags in his hand. "I found these on the port deck next to the bridge, Captain Rogers. Port watch said they saw a man standing there for a few moments, then he was not visible. He must have jumped overboard!"

Captain Rogers accepted the tags and read the name: "These belong to a Major Donald Markey."

Nathan heard the name, Major Donald Markey, and turned white with shock, and cried aloud: "My God... Dr. Donald Markey."

He left the wardroom and ran to the deck, bending over a rail to empty his stomach...!

Chapter Eighteen

Summer 1951

Even now, six years after the incident, Nathan felt the same anguish he experienced that day when he should have been celebrating a very successful event. Twenty-three American soldiers had just been snatched from the jaws of death. No other incident in his long and active career in the Coast Guard ever compared to the emotional upheaval caused by Dr. Donald Markey's suicide. His first thought was that if he had handled the doctor's conduct differently, maybe he would not have taken his own life. Nathan had shamed him and mocked him when he should have shown more compassion for a man on the edge of a volcano about to erupt.

Captain Rogers had lowered two lifeboats to search the area for the man's body. They found nothing. Donald Markey had perished in the dark blue waters of the Pacific. The question of why had been a part of Nathan's consciousness ever since, causing great inner turmoil.

The years had passed quickly since the surrender of the Japanese. He had been proud to have been present at the Japanese surrender ceremony, August 15, 1945, on the deck of the battleship *USS Missouri*. The *Northland* had acted as an escort to the battleship and stationed itself on the port side of the ship in Tokyo Bay where they witnessed the surrender ceremony.

That fall, Nathan arrived home with a month furlough, uncertain what he wanted to do with his life. He used the furlough to make up his mind whether he wanted to stay in the Coast Guard or seek employment in the civilian workplace. He found that jobs were scarce with the influx of millions of young men being mustered out of the services. No civilian job was capable of paying as much as his salary in the Coast Guard, so he decided that he was going to stay in for at least twenty years before retirement.

The prolonged furlough gave him a chance to get better acquainted with Lena. He enjoyed her company at a few movies. They seemed to get along without discourse. One evening they had gone to a theatre in Belfast to see *Going My Way* with Bing Crosby. After the movie, they went to the local diner for a cup of coffee and a piece of apple pie. Lena had been uncharacteristically quieter than usual all evening.

Nathan had asked her, "You're quiet tonight, Lena. Is anything wrong?"

She turned to look at him. "No, nothing is wrong. I've just been wondering about the future. I plan to keep my job as a teacher. Your mother and Casey are doing fine in the old house. I'm thinking of moving back into my old apartment which is available."

"You've been a great help to Ma and me. Casey adores you," Nathan had told her. "I've decided to stay in the Coast Guard. I talked it over with Ma. It places an added burden on her, but she seems to want to continue with the way things are. Casey's five-years-old and starts school this fall. I feel a little guilty about the responsibility she's taking off my shoulders and don't see any other way out of the situation. I'm hoping to get a post along the Maine coastline so that I can be home more often."

"It would be nice to see more of you," she replied, turning away from him. "I know that I'm acting bold, but do you and I have a future, Nathan?"

The question came filled with expectations and an air of uncertainty. He was reluctant to give her the answer she was hoping for. "Oh, Lena, I do like you, and I respect you very much. For now, would it be enough to just be friends? To be honest, I'm not prepared to say that we do or do not have a future. I say that, not because there is someone else in my life, it's just that I have got to unwind a lot of things that have happened during this war that will take some time before I take on any emotional commitments. I know it's not the answer you wanted to hear, but it's an honest evaluation of my feelings."

The disappointment was sobering for her. "I understand your position and appreciate your honesty. I was hoping for something different, yet I can accept the reality of the situation. It's getting late. We should be getting home, Nate."

Lena and Nathan saw very little of each other after she moved to her apartment. She rarely spoke to him about her feelings. The warmth they once felt had dissipated. He felt bad because she was a good person, and he did not want to hurt her in any way. In time, she found a wonderful guy who married her two years later. Their marriage relieved him of a lot of guilt.

Nathan continued to serve in the Coast Guard along the Atlantic seaboard. He was able to get home quite often to see Casey and his mother. He went fishing and hunting with Casey and was able to attend some of his son's school baseball games. It had been an idyllic time with Casey at the center of his life. Then, on June 25, 1950 the distant war drums called him again to combat on the other side of the world. This time it was Korea!

He was assigned to the naval contingent sent to Korea to conduct an amphibious operation at a place called Inchon. The Coast Guard cutter with its shallow draft was assigned the task of eliminating enemy installations on several of the small islands around the port of Inchon prior to the assault. The Navy always valued the ability of the Coast Guard to launch ad hoc shore parties. Nathan was selected to lead the Coast Guard contingent to operate with a platoon of Navy infantry under the command of a Lieutenant Clark. The small group quickly began to clear several of the smaller islands of Korean forces. It was conducted at a rapid pace because time was of the essence. The large amphibious force of Marines could only land at high tides. The fighting was intense for the Koreans knew what was at stake. One of the largest islands had an airfield with several planes that held a real threat to the Marine landings. Nathan and his squad of Coast Guardsmen were given the task of eliminating the planes with bazookas. He had taken out three planes with the rocket firing weapon when he was wounded by a mortar round that knocked him unconscious.

When he woke up from the explosion, he was on a Navy ship in a large ward filled with wounded men. He was heavily drugged and remembered going in and out of consciousness. His upper torso was tightly wrapped with bandages, and his right leg was suspended in the air with small wires. There was no pain. He could move his right arm, but when he tried to move his left arm he felt no response. Straining to look at his arm, he saw an empty sleeve! A howling cry of despair pierced his lips! It was a painful discovery. The reality that he was going to live the rest of his life with only one arm made him feel like a cripple.

Nathan was shipped back to the states for recovery and physical therapy treatment so that he could learn to manipulate an artificial arm. He selected the Navy hospital at Brunswick, Maine for his therapy. Weeks of intense therapy were necessary for him to use his new arm. In time he would become very proficient with the new addition to his body, but many discouraging days were ahead of him. Months later he was discharged from the hospital and the Coast Guard with a disability monthly payment.

Returning home in what he believed was an incomplete human body, he soon learned to accept his condition without rancor. He now had a goal ahead of him. During his recovery period, Nathan reviewed potential career possibilities, and he selected forestry. He had always loved the forest. The things he had read about the forest management program on the large holdings of the Great Northern Paper Company in northern Maine fascinated him. As a veteran of World War Two and of the Korean War, he was entitled to the benefits of the generous G.I. Bill of Rights: a bill passed to assist veterans in getting a college education. It was one of the most generous and successful pieces of legislation ever passed.

Several times he had an opportunity to work with the Marine Laboratory of the University of New Hampshire while conducting fish population studies around the Isle of Shoals. He decided to apply for admittance at the university in Durham, New Hampshire, and was accepted. He planned to rent an apartment and move in with his son, Casey. It was his turn to take responsibility. His mother moved into an assisted living home in Belfast. Her legs were bothering her in getting around. She was unhappy for a while but once she learned that several of her friends also lived at the facility, she resigned herself to let others help her.

The bright, sunny day that Nathan and Casey left Belfast for Durham, Nathan could not pass by Wells without stopping to reminisce about a time in his life he yearned to discover again. Casey searched among the rocks on the shore of Wells Beach for crabs and starfish. Nathan turned to look at the old Coast Guard station on the hill facing the beach and reminisced about happier times. He was having a hard time letting go. A whole new life was ahead of him, and if it was to be a happy one, he had to say goodbye and close the door on the past.

Twelve-year-old Casey had watched his father deep in thought and was worried about him. "Are you okay, Dad?"

Nathan nodded his head to break the reverie, and turned wistfully toward his son. "I was just thinking about another time and another life when I was younger, son. The past becomes very precious to a person as they get older. You'll find that out for yourself. Come let's continue to Durham and check out our new apartment."

He slowly drove by the old observation tower and the renovated barrack building. Visions of old friends filled his heart. Some were now gone forever. The image that stayed with him the longest was that of Dr. Colleen Markey. It was as strong as ever, yet he knew that he had to put the past behind him. When he turned south on Route One a moist film covered his vision. Saying goodbye was not an easy task!

Their apartment was just off the university campus. It was a wooden complex built to hold the large influx of veterans to the campus. Casey was enrolled in the seventh grade in Durham. Shortly after settling into their new surroundings, Nathan purchased a brand new 1951 Studebaker Land Cruiser with an automatic transmission and a powerful V/8 engine. It was painted a beautiful black cherry color. It was one of the few times in his life that he splurged and bought something for himself. He loved to drive it. With his artificial arm it was easier to not have to shift the transmission.

The forestry course at the University of New Hampshire was a four-year curriculum with a Bachelor of Arts degree awarded at graduation. Nathan dove into the demanding schedule with his usual disciplined commitment. He was thirty-eight years old and saw this as the last chance to improve his life. He carried twenty semester credits for the first semester. Adapting to the learning routine was not easy. He made it a point of always being home when Casey got out of school. They attended sporting events at the college on a regular basis. Casey especially liked basketball.

One day he was walking past the auditorium where he heard music being played by an orchestra. Nathan walked into the amphitheater and watched the University symphony orchestra rehearse. He loved music and stopped to listen to it for several minutes before leaving to visit the library. An hour later he left the library and passed by the auditorium on his way to the apartment. Passing by an open window he heard the plaintive sound of a cello being played. Out of curiosity he stepped into the auditorium and saw a single figure intensely bent over a cello playing one of his all-time favorite melodies, *Londonderry Aire.* He took a seat and closed his eyes listening to the sad refrain. The experience sent shivers up and down his spine. The last few bars of the song were pure rapture. The person playing the instrument sat back in her chair and was quiet for several seconds.

Nathan stood up and walked towards the stage. "I was listening from the back of the auditorium. Your rendition of that old Irish favorite was beautiful. I really enjoyed it."

The lady placed her cello against the stand and turned to him. "Thank you. It's my favorite. The poignancy of its message still brings tears to my eyes. I haven't had much time to practice since school started," she replied, stepping down from the stage. "Do you play an instrument?"

He smiled and said, "No, I don't play anything, I never had much time to take up an instrument. Besides, a cripple with an arm like this would find it difficult."

She quickly stepped in front of him and placed a finger across his lips, angrily replying, "Hush, now. You're not a cripple. You're simply disabled, and most everybody is disabled in some way or another, some physically and some emotionally. I'm a disabled person, but I could never call myself a cripple and neither should you," she cried forcefully, lifting the pant leg of her slacks on her left leg to show that it was an artificial one.

He was stunned by the ferocity of her response. "Lady, I apologize for the remark. I meant it more as a joke than a complaint of my condition. I agree wholeheartedly with your statement. I only wanted to show the limitation on playing an instrument of any kind," he replied with a smile.

She smiled back at him. "As you can see, I have strong feelings about the word cripple. You're new on campus, aren't you?"

"Yes, I just enrolled in the forestry curriculum. I'm thankful for the chance to get an education. Incidentally, my name is Nathan Collins."

"Welcome to Durham, Nathan. My name is Alita Larochelle. I'm studying for a degree in music. I was an Army nurse in Italy when my Jeep ran over a land mine. I try not to think about it; it could have been worse."

"There are still times when I have sessions of self-pity, but I'm getting better. I got hit in Korea last year, so I've got a little longer to adapt. Well, it's been nice talking with you, Alita. My son will be coming home from school soon. See you around campus. Your playing is inspiring, really."

"Thanks, Nathan. You're welcome to sit in on our practice sessions anytime."

"I'd like that. Goodbye."

Within a week Nathan and Casey had settled into the academic routine of the university. One weekend in October, they drove up to the White Mountains where they checked on the Old Man of the Mountain through a pair of binoculars. The foliage was just beginning to change, painting a magnificent tapestry of color across the landscape. They camped out Saturday night and returned to the campus Sunday. As they drove past the auditorium Nathan noted a few cars parked in the parking lot. He asked Casey if he would like to listen to some pretty music.

"Sure, Dad, I like music. I liked it when Grandmother and Aunt Lena played the piano at home."

"Well, if you enjoyed one instrument, you'll like to hear the full orchestra with an array of different instruments," Nathan said, getting out of the Studebaker.

There were a couple of dozen people in the auditorium listening to the practice session of the orchestra. They were doing a large number of current popular songs such as *Mona Lisa, Goodnight Irene, Riders in the Sky, Cry, and Shrimp Boats Are Coming*. They also did *Bouquet of Roses* and a segment of Beethoven's *Sixth Symphony*. The latter describes a country setting very much like New Hampshire's rural makeup. Nathan spotted Alita in the front row closest to the audience. She had a relaxed air about her while she played and often closed her eyes. She had short sandy hair pulled back behind her ears. Once when she looked out at the audience she smiled at Nathan and Casey.

The conductor drew the practice session to a close reminding the members to mark their calendars for next week's performance. Alita carefully placed her cello and bow into her case and walked off the stage, heading towards Nathan and Casey. Two women had been sitting behind Nathan during the practice session. They approached him first. Out of nowhere, a familiar figure held out her arms to Nathan, "I thought that was you, Chief," cried Dr. Colleen Markey!

Chapter Nineteen

1952-University of New Hampshire

Nathan was speechless as he embraced the lovely Dr. Markey there in front of an auditorium filled with people. Casey gave his father a puzzled look. "To say that I'm surprised, Dr. Markey, would be the understatement of the year."

"It's so good to know that you survived the two wars, Chief," she exclaimed, releasing him to introduce the two ladies with her. "This is my cousin, Andrea, and this is also my cousin, Alita."

He shook hands with them and introduced his son, Casey. "We were attracted to the wonderful music coming from the auditorium. My, what a surprise. The last time I saw you was on a hospital ship in the Pacific Ocean. It's a small world."

Alita saw how shocked and self-conscious he was meeting Dr. Markey in such a public place. "Listen, girls. I have an idea. Andrea and I will scoot along. We can meet you later at the restaurant in the middle of town. If Casey would like to join us he can help me carry the cello to my car."

Nathan was glad to get the chance to be alone with the good doctor. As soon as they left, he turned to her, saying, "Would you mind if we went outside to my car, Doctor?" he asked. "I have to talk to you."

She saw how important it was for him and agreed. "If you wish, Chief. I think both of us need to talk in private. I must say that I did not know you came to the University of New Hampshire until I saw you walk down the aisle of the auditorium. I'm sorry about your arm. Where did it happen?"

"I lost it in Korea off Inchon. I'm doing okay though. Compared to some vets, I'm fortunate. I'm taking advantage of the education offered to all veterans and enrolled in the forestry program here at the University. Casey and I rented an apartment for the four years." He linked his right arm around hers and directed her to the Studebaker.

His mind was so jumbled that he was having trouble thinking straight. Her presence had completely disarmed him. If he was not careful he could make a fool of himself. How he ached to hold her in his arms and tell her he loved her!

Colleen Markey was a shrewd reader of human conduct and saw clearly what was clouding his head. She vowed to not let his feelings deny reality, for that would be even more painful in the long run. She hoped she could do that to this courageous man without breaking his spirit or his belief in his fellow man. Once they closed the Studebaker's doors, the silence was deafening. Nathan self-consciously rolled his driver side window down. He was the first to speak.

"There are two issues I need to discuss with you now that we have a chance to share what has been a terrible burden for me to carry. At times, I wondered if I was going out of my mind and didn't really care if that took place."

She grasped his right hand and the hook he had fashioned to the end of his new arm, and turned to face him. "Oh, Nathan, am I really responsible for such heavy burdens? I'm so proud of you and have cherished you as a friend. What is it that has burdened you the most? Please be honest. Tell me the truth."

"Number one is that I fell in love with you in Wells, and could never shake the ache I carried everywhere I went. I know that what you counseled was wise advice, but I lacked the strength to control the sentiments that grew stronger and stronger." He shook his head in amazement that he was confessing such feelings. "And I was the man who took pride in my ability to discipline myself. I saw your face in everything I did. You were with me in those darkest hours when I drew sustenance from your strength. I knew, oh I knew, that I was out of bounds, but it didn't matter. You simply became an obsession to me."

153

"I saw some of what you describe, and I hope that I did not give you false hope. I also had to fight feelings that were strong and a violation of sacred vows. In time, I controlled them and faced reality with open eyes," she honestly declared.

"How easy it was to fuel the flames of destruction," he continued. "I never was a lovesick teenager. No one ever made me feel the way I did for you. On top of all that, the task force I led to free some prisoners not only elevated my respect for my fellow Americans, it also made me angry with my own actions. My treatment and lack of compassion for your husband, Major Donald Markey, has been a memory I can't escape from..."

He was getting more and more distraught as the revelations poured from his soul. Unable to control the force of his emotions, he wept openly, holding his head on his right arm against the steering wheel of the Studebaker.

Dr. Colleen Markey sat helplessly beside Nathan. He needed this release, as heart-wrenching as it was to witness. It was a cathartic experience that purged some of the pain and guilt he had harbored for so long.

"My dear Nathan, you carried a burden of guilt that was so unnecessary. From the very beginning, my husband was a weak man. Even in medical school I had to constantly encourage him and help him. I must tell you that I had a long discussion with Captain Jones on our hospital ship. He told me everything that happened. My husband betrayed me, his men, our country, and himself to the point where he could not live with the consequences he was about to face. He was a coward among heroes. It's a tribute to the integrity of those soldiers who did not seek revenge on him for his obsessive concern of self."

Nathan listened to the calm reasoning of her soft voice. The things she was telling him about her husband rang true. It was as he had expected. He reached in his pocket for a handkerchief to dry his eyes and blow his nose. In a shaky voice he told her: "I became so angry at the man that I threw him in a river. God, I'd take that act back if I could."

"Would you please do something for me, Chief?" she questioned with a light touch on his arm.

"You have but to ask..."

"I want you to erase all of those ugly images from your mind. I think your actions were appropriate under the circumstances. My husband was simply too weak to own up to what he had done during his imprisonment. You had nothing to do with that. I do not judge you for any action. To the contrary, Captain Jones and all of the men you saved from extinction have nothing but praise for the actions of you and your men. They saw what I've always seen in you, Chief. I've always been proud of you... Now, having said that, you must know that I am engaged to marry a wonderful man who has won my heart. If that fact hurts, then God forgive me, but you have a right to the truth. I'm hoping that my best friend, Chief Petty Officer Nathan Collins, would wish me well and share my happiness. Do you think that might be possible?"

Nathan nodded his head at her request. "Of course I wish you well. I apologize for falling apart like this. Thanks for being so supportive. You deserve the very best, Lady. He's a lucky man. I do share your happiness; I half expected such a thing to happen. Now that we've been honest with each other, I want you to know that I, too, will honor our friendship. How can I describe it?" he paused, holding her two hands. "I feel as if a heavy load has just been removed. Thanks for helping me face reality. I came here to the university to start a new life for me and Casey. Thanks for releasing me from the bonds that have been so painful for a long time."

She embraced him with tears of happiness running down her cheeks. "How fortunate we are to have men like you to protect this great land of ours. I hope Casey grows up to be like his dad."

Nathan knew that the two of them had reached a milestone in their relationship, a level of intimacy that few people experience. It wasn't what he had hoped for, but he could accept it without rancor or regret. The future now belonged to him, and with friends like the gentle soft-spoken lady at his side, how could he fail?

"I'm a very lucky man. Thanks for being honest with me. Are you as hungry as I am?"

"Yes," she replied. "Let's join Casey and the girls before the restaurant closes."

Two years later, Nathan was beginning his third year at the university. It had taken him a while to adapt to the academic routine. He had often attended training sessions in the Coast Guard. He was no stranger to a classroom, having acted as an instructor to the men he was responsible for. The forestry curriculum included more math and chemistry than he had anticipated. Those courses required more effort on his part than the forestry subjects such as forest management, mensuration, silvics and statistics.

During the past summer, Nathan searched for and obtained employment on campus with the Agricultural Experiment Station so that he could keep his apartment. He had traveled to Belfast to visit his mother as often as his busy schedule permitted. She was doing fine with several long-standing friends in the same facility.

He had occasionally seen Alita Larochelle on campus. One day after his conversation with Dr. Markey, he sat with Alita at the Commons Cafeteria eating lunch. She had told him that her cousin Colleen had recently married and was starting a practice in central Maine. The news was not unexpected. He accepted the fact better than anticipated. Alita had watched him closely and remarked: "Colleen deserves some happiness. Her first husband was a terrible disappointment to her."

"How well did you know him, Alita?" he casually asked.

"She met him at school. I only saw him at her wedding. I was her bridesmaid and had just graduated from nursing school before the war. I judged him to be one of those likeable eccentrics you see on many of our campuses. She seemed happy, so we all wished her the best. Colleen told me about your rescue of the prisoners," Alita mentioned.

"He definitely had a problem. I was pretty harsh on him. At the time I suspected that he had selfishly taken the path of least resistance in the prison camp. As an officer he had an obligation to take care of the men. As a physician, his duty was even more pressing," Nathan declared, surprised that he could talk so openly about the incident.

Alita slowly drank the rest of her coffee, telling him she had to make a class. He had the feeling that she was somewhat of a loner. She had a wide circle of friends who saw her as a happy-go-lucky person who did not take herself seriously. Over the past two years, Nathan had the opportunity to catch glimpses of her in a different light. He came to the conclusion that she was hiding a lot of sadness. She always wore a wedding ring on her finger, but never mentioned a husband. She had occasionally helped Casey with some of his homework and had introduced him to music. She had a violin she let him borrow if he promised to be serious about taking lessons on the instrument. She volunteered her services twice a week meeting at their apartment.

One summer day after Casey's lesson, he left the apartment to play baseball. Nathan was just sitting down to a late lunch and offered to fix her a sandwich and coffee.

"A peanut butter and jelly sandwich would taste good," she replied in a good mood. She joked about several of her friends who would be interested in going out with him.

He laughed and replied: "You surprise me, Alita. I'm thirty-eight years old, hardly a teenager." He used the light banter to bring up a subject she never ventured into on her own. "I could say the same thing about you, young lady. If I'm out of line, please tell me to mind my own business. I see that you wear a wedding ring. Where is your husband?"

She winced and looked away. The question had penetrated her defenses. "My husband was killed at Normandy in 1944. We grew up together and fell in love. I still cherish his memory. The ring makes a statement to the world that I'm not unattached, besides, this wooden leg discourages romantic entanglements…"

Ah! She was using the ring to shield her from unpleasant reactions to her condition. "Alita, I find that answer unsatisfactory. Sure, it's only fitting and normal that we respect the memories of those who have gone on. How do you know that a potential suitor might be turned off by an artificial limb?" he asked, hoping that he did not take the conversation into unwelcome waters.

She was not happy with his statement. "I've seen how a few are turned off. They become too conciliatory and make excuses that they have another appointment or an errand to run. Oh, yes, I've seen enough to substantiate my statement. This conversation is becoming heavy, Nathan."

"I'm sorry, Alita. I was going to ask you if you'd like to join Casey and me in a ride up to the White Mountains. The foliage should be at a peak right now up there. I have to go up every once in a while just to be sure they're still there. Just being in the presence of all that beauty and grandeur makes me feel whole and insignificant. Tomorrow morning we plan to go up Route 16 to North Conway to have lunch. Weather forecast is for a sunny day tomorrow. How about it, Alita? It'll give you a chance to see how the Studebakers eat up the road." He had often kidded her about her Chevrolet coupe with special hand controls for brake and clutch operation.

She returned his grin. "You make a powerful argument for an affirmative answer, Nathan. I haven't been up to the mountains since I was a little girl in grade school. I didn't mean to be so negative about my condition."

"I know that. Your husband would be proud of you, young lady. Those who judge or rate people like us should be avoided. We don't need them in our lives. That first time I heard you play the cello, I felt privileged to have experienced the beauty you portrayed through the music. If we were graded on what's in our hearts, you, my dear friend, would be at the top of the list. So… don't give me anymore negatives about your misfortune. Understood?"

Her eyes moistened, and she kissed him on the cheek. "Thank you for telling me that, Chief."

The next morning, Nathan started the Studebaker and headed for the North Country with Alita sitting up front. Casey took the back seat with a supply of comic books. Destination: North Conway for lunch. It was a relief for all of them to get away from the campus for a while. It was a warm, sunny day in September. They were in an expansive mood looking forward to a pleasant drive. Nathan loved to drive the Studebaker. He faithfully washed and waxed it on a regular basis.

Alita impishly remarked that the Studebaker did ride nice and quiet. "That automatic transmission is a wonderful idea. It eliminates the need for constant shifts. How much extra was it over a regular transmission, Nathan?"

"I think it was about two hundred dollars more. Would you like to try it?" he asked, pulling off into a rest area.

She was a little shy. "I really like to drive. If you don't mind, I'll take it for a few miles. I may not want to go back to my converted Chevy," she laughed.

"You'll never know unless you try something different," he said, getting out of the driver's seat so that she could slide into it. He took the seat beside her and pointed to the selector dial on the shift lever. "The shift patterns are not so very different as you have on a standard like your Chevy. The numbers are obvious. All you have to do is place your foot on the brake pedal and move the lever to whatever gear you want. 'D' is for normal forward travel. You'll feel the transmission make the shifts as you speed up. You stop just like your Chevy, except you don't have any clutch. Once at a stop, you place the lever in 'P' for park. That's all there is to it. Use your right foot exactly as you do on your Chevy. I think you'll like it. All of the car makers are offering an automatic transmission now."

Alita concentrated on her sitting position in the Studebaker, adjusting the mirrors to suit her. She self-consciously pulled the shift lever to 'D' and released the brake. The vehicle was a lot more responsive than her Chevy. She checked both ways and pulled out into the traffic lane.

A smile came across her lips. "This is such a nice car to drive, Nathan. It would be easy to speed with it."

"If you get a speeding ticket," he chuckled, "You pay for it, Lady. You know this being chauffeured around by a lovely lady could be addictive."

She quickly glanced at him. "Thank you for asking me to spend the day with you and Casey."

Nathan had a chance to study her up close while she drove north up Route 16. Most of the time he had known her she was a serious person. She smiled more today than he had noticed. She wore her coal-black hair short, pulled behind her ears with a red barrette holding it off her forehead. Dressed in a light purple blouse with dark purple slacks, she projected an air of confidence whether she was driving a vehicle or playing her cello. Her ability to focus with intensity with whatever she was doing, helped to define her. Nathan detected a subtle aroma of perfume like a wild rose. He thought that she was the kind of woman a person could know for a long time and still discover something new everyday.

They arrived at North Conway, stopping at a small restaurant north of the town with a wonderful view of Mount Washington and the cog railroad that climbed to the top of the mountain. The panorama was alive with splashes of red and yellow hues against the dark blue sky. The view left all of them in a pensive and reflective mood. To say that it was beautiful was an understatement.

Nathan looked across the table at Alita, noting a moist film clouding her vision. He reached across the table and squeezed her hands as if to say, "I understand." It was a quiet interlude that touched their consciousness.

Alita was the first to break the silence. "Beauty always brings tears. This has been a wonderful day. To share the magnificence of the mountains at this time of year with you and Casey has been very special. Thanks again for letting me tag along."

It was a poignant moment of discovery in their relationship. For the past two years, their relationship had grown into a warm friendship that each felt secure and comfortable with. During their trip to the mountains, something different had taken place, leaving both of them quite unprepared to recognize what had taken place.

That night Nathan dropped her off at her apartment, escorting her to the door. She reached for her keys and said, "This has been a wonderful day for me, Nathan. I'm not sure what has passed between us, but today, for the first time, I recognized that something was missing in my life. Feelings have a way of creeping up on a person…" She nervously wiped a tear from her eye.

Nathan too was aware of stirrings of the heart. "Let's give it some time, Alita…" He took her into his arms and kissed her. She clasped her arms around him and softly cried…

Chapter Twenty

1953 - University of New Hampshire

During the Christmas break of 1953, Nathan and Casey went home to Belfast to spend some time with Nathan's mother who was not doing very well. She had broken a rib during a fall and was uncomfortable. It was a shock to see how much his mother had deteriorated since his last visit. She was unable to carry on a conversation. Her mind wandered and several times she asked who he was. They left the facility with mixed emotions when she fell asleep. Casey remarked how she had bad color and was slow to respond to their questions.

"You've got to remember, Casey, that your grandmother is getting older just like us. I want to check on the condition of the house," Nathan explained for their sudden departure from the nursing home.

He had a premonition that time was running out on the courageous lady who had held the family together when the world was crumbling around her.

The old house was desperately in need of a paint job and portions of the deck had rotted away. His father had been faithful in maintaining the homestead in good repair. Nathan felt guilty that he had neglected those necessities. Three feet of snow now covered the driveway. Water had been turned off to prevent frozen pipes from bursting. After a quick check on the interior, they returned to the Studebaker parked beside the road. As for Nathan, it was difficult to walk away from something that was so much a part of his life.

They returned to learn that his mother was resting. The staff nurse told him that she was withdrawing more and more from reality. He understood, for she did not recognize him or Casey on their previous visit. He stood over her and reluctantly made the decision to return to Durham. Leaning over his sleeping mother, Nathan kissed her on the temple and sadly left the facility.

It was a long trip. The minute he left the nursing home, he knew it was the last time he would see her alive. Echoes from the past flooded through his mind bringing back events of happier days that could never be duplicated. He was glad that Casey had fallen asleep on the seat beside him. Several times on the trip to Durham tears ran down his cheeks obstructing his vision. He quickly wiped them away, choked with grief that there was nothing he could do except pray. Her place in Heaven was assured. He prayed to be worthy of all of the sacrifices his mother made for the family.

It was late in the evening when he turned into their apartment parking lot. Casey quickly climbed into bed after a quick ham and cheese sandwich, leaving Nathan alone in the kitchen with his thoughts. He had just put on a pot of coffee when a light knock sounded at the front door. He opened it for Alita.

"I was leaving the orchestra practice session when I saw your Studebaker in the parking lot. I didn't expect you until tomorrow. Is anything wrong?" she asked in a hushed tone.

"Come in, Alita. I know it's late…" he said, embracing her. "We left my mother with regrets. She's doing poorly. Come and sit down. Do you want a cup of coffee?" he asked, motioning for her to take a seat at the small table.

She saw the dark lines around his sad eyes and winced at the haunting stare that he shared with most war veterans. "I'll have a small one, Nathan. I'm sorry to hear about your mother. Is she being well cared for?"

"I think so. Several of her friends are in the same facility. When she was more mobile I had the feeling that she liked it there," he explained. "As a matter of fact, seeing how well the nurses handled the patients made me wonder why you didn't return to your nursing career. If I'm out of bounds, I withdraw my question. I'm glad to see you tonight."

She placed a spoon of sugar in her coffee and stirred it. "You make a good cup of coffee. I would expect that from a seasoned Coastie," she smiled. "You ask what Colleen and the rest of my family have been questioning me about. The time I spent in the Army field hospitals introduced me to the unspeakable horrors that hot steel can do to human bodies. When I lost my leg in the mine explosion, I also lost my hearing and vision. In time both returned, but I can tell you in all honesty that my hearing is still not as good as it should be. It took about a year. I have to wear glasses to read now."

"I'm sorry, I didn't mean to drudge up bad thoughts," Nathan exclaimed.

"When I was first discharged from the Army," she continued, "I was unable to perform the duties of a nurse, so I decided to take advantage of the college courses made available to veterans. Music has always been one of my passions. If I can't make a living with my music, I'll return to nursing. I've maintained my certification since I've been at school."

While she had been talking, Nathan saw a different person. By nature she was modest and serious. He often saw her impish and spontaneous, but tonight he saw her slightly withdrawn and hesitant to talk about her career as a nurse. She looked tired.

"Are you all right, Alita?" he asked.

"This has been a busy week for me," she explained. "I've used my cousin Colleen as my primary physician since I left the Army. I plan to see her this coming weekend. She wants to check on my blood sugar level. Our family has a history of diabetes, so she wants to be on top of that."

"Well, you're in good hands," he replied, pondering her statement.

"Colleen and I have always been close. She's a little older than me. She was a lot of help when I lost my husband. I can now tell you that she told me what had passed between the two of you," she explained hesitantly.

"I have much respect for your cousin. Her memory sustained me through the war. The last conversation we had here in Durham was not too difficult. I always knew I was reaching for something that was unobtainable. In some ways it was a relief for me to face reality. I hope we can still remain friends," Nathan confessed.

"You'll be pleased to know that she and her new husband are very happy together. Her relationship with Major Markey was all one-sided. I never liked him," she said, preparing to leave. "I am tired. I'm going to bed as soon as I get to my apartment."

"That sounds like a good idea, Alita," he said, taking her in his arms. "I'll see you when you get back from Maine. I'll miss you."

"It's nice to be missed," she said, returning his kiss. "Tell Casey we'll double up on his lessons next week when I return. I love you, Nathan."

"It's easy to say 'I love you' when the words are true," he smiled, walking her to the door and out to her Chevy with an arm around her. "Have a safe trip. Road conditions can be treacherous at this time of year. Until next time."

"Until next time," she waved as she turned the corner out of sight.

Seeing her disappear made him feel alone and incomplete. Ever since their trip in September to the White Mountains Nathan had fallen more and more in love with the sensitive and illusive lady who cried so easily when she played beautiful music or viewed a beautiful scene. Without pretense or fanfare she had captured his heart. She was always there with encouragement and support when he need it to get through some of his more difficult forestry courses.

Casey adored her, telling his father that she was a tough instructor who settled only for maximum effort on the violin. Slowly under Alita's demanding tutelage, Casey had developed a passion for music and was becoming a fine violin player. Music had helped him bridge the gap between childhood and adolescence. It gave him poise and self-confidence.

That Christmas, Nathan planned to spend some time with his mother in Belfast. Two days prior to his departure from Durham, the nursing home informed him that she had passed away peacefully in her sleep. The news was not unexpected, but it devastated his self-control. Anxious to make arrangements for her funeral, he and Casey left to open up the old homestead and to reconnect the telephone line. Plans for his mother's funeral and eventual burial at Belfast were readily made as soon as they arrived in town.

Nathan's trip to the funeral home to pick out a casket was one of the most difficult things he ever did. Old friends, and there were many in the small community, came to pay their respect. Several neighbors and friends supplied the home with a large assortment of food that overflowed from the large kitchen table. He was appreciative, but food did not appeal to him. Lena and her husband urged him to eat something to maintain strength for the ordeal ahead of him.

The day of the funeral, Alita arrived with Colleen and her new husband, Joel Atkins. He was anxious to see her again just to make sure that he had effectively dealt with the fascination he had for her over the years. It was refreshing to greet her as a friend. The old feelings had a lot of guilt attached to them. Seeing her again with her husband was the reality that he needed. He had passed the test...

Filled with grief and running on nerves, Nathan was pleased to see Alita. He embraced her warmly and silently wept in her arms. The wake at the funeral home was the hardest to bear. Hundreds of friends and acquaintances over the years filed past the open casket, shaking hands with Casey and Nathan. Lena, Alita, and Colleen and her husband sat silently by, observing the outpouring of love and respect.

Nathan had the urge to tell everyone to go home and leave him alone. Small talk just about drove him crazy. The service at the church was brief. He badly needed the chance to be alone to say good-bye to his mother. Colleen and her husband left shortly after the service.

Lena invited Alita to stay with her after the funeral if she wished. Alita appreciated the offer, but seeing how Nathan needed some time to be alone, she suggested that she take Casey back to Durham with her. Nathan agreed with the arrangement, asking them to take some of the foodstuff at the old house. Alita and Casey reluctantly left him at such a turbulent time. He insisted that he would be all right; he simply needed some space to realign his life and would be home in a few days.

Once he was alone, he drove out to a location he had frequently gone to when he wanted to think through some problem or to simply be alone. He was a man who required some solitude in his life. Perhaps it was what had made the Arctic so appealing to him. He carefully drove the Studebaker out over a recently plowed roadway that led to the tip end of a peninsula with a panoramic view of the Atlantic Ocean at the mouth of the Penobscot River.

The tide was high. He watched the restless wave's splash against the granite shore. The energy of the continuous assault matched the turbulence within his life, yet he felt a peace he had not experienced for days. The sea always had a calming influence on him. He could still picture his father boarding the faithful ferry boat for its rounds to the small islands off the coast of Maine. He had been blessed with a wonderful childhood with two parents that loved and cherished him. Fond memories were numerous and often brought a smile to his lips.

He sat at the coast for a couple of hours before he turned the Studebaker around to leave. His headlights shined on a "for sale" sign beside the roadway. Suddenly he was moved to write down the telephone number of the owner. That generated something deep within him that he had just now contemplated. The prospect that he might be able to purchase the site he had often visited, ignited his curiosity to explore the potential.

As soon as he returned to the house in Belfast, he called the number on the sign. The phone rang several times before a voice answered, "Hello."

"Hello, this is Nathan Collins. I'm calling about the piece of land out on Penobscot Bay."

"I thought it was you, Chief. I saw your mother's obituary in the paper. You have my sympathy. This is Matthew Rogers."

The voice sounded familiar. "Thanks, Captain Rogers. It's a small world. I didn't know that you lived in Maine."

"I'm visiting some of my mother's family in the area. I knew that you were injured in Korea and had entered college. It's nice to hear from you. The piece of land you refer to belongs to my nephew. He's asking $3,000.00 for the ten acres. I went out there the day before Christmas. My, what a lovely site for a home. Are you an interested buyer, Chief?"

"Yes and no, Captain. This has been a rough period for me. Somewhere in the back of my mind there's a desire to own a waterfront property in Maine. I don't have that kind of money available right now. I've got another year and a half of school to finish. What would it take for your nephew to give me first refusal on the property if he has another offer, sir?"

"Chief Collins, if you're seriously interested in the property, your word is enough for me. Your record of courage and dedication to this country is a legacy that is priceless. I will gladly vouch for you."

"I appreciate that, Captain Rogers. Tell your nephew that I'll be in touch as soon as I settle some of my family affairs. It was nice talking to an old shipmate. Semper Paratus, Sir."

"You took the words out of my mouth. Semper Paratus, Chief Collins."

That evening Nathan sat down to a plate of baked beans and brown bread with a hot cup of coffee. It was his first full meal since he left Durham. The phone rang while he was eating. "Hello," he said.

"Nathan, this is Alita. I'm calling just to be sure you're all right. You looked so sad and forlorn when we left. I'll sleep on the couch tonight. Casey just went to bed. He was exhausted and worried over you. He's a fine young man very much like his dad. I miss you, Nathan."

"I miss you too, Alita. I'm glad you called. I was worried about road conditions. We're getting a few flurries here now."

"We made good time, stopping in Portsmouth to have a light lunch. I'll be staying here with Casey until you return. Take as long as you need. Until next time, Nathan, I love you."

"I love you, too, Alita. The minute you and Casey left, I missed you. How lucky I am to be loved by such a lovely lady. Goodnight, my love."

Nathan took another day to close up the house and to drain the water pipes for the winter months. Uncertain about the future, he stopped by a local realtor's office to obtain an approximate value of the house and to tentatively place it on the market. Immediately after, he went to thank Lena and her husband for all their support. He told both of them about what he had done with the house and also about the piece of land on the waterfront. They were more up-to-date on local land prices and values, and offered to show the house to the realtor if he had an interested buyer. Lena's husband, Jake, told him the price for the ten acres sounded like a good buy. With that good news ringing in his ears, he headed for Durham with the faithful Studebaker.

Chapter Twenty-One

Embracing The Future

Nathan and Alita saw each other every day after the New Year. He observed a very subtle decline in her enthusiasm for her music. She seemed tired and weary most of the time. Even Casey noted the change. Dark circles developed under her eyes. One morning she almost fainted while sitting at the kitchen table sharing a cup of coffee and a piece of toast with Nathan. She caught herself in time by quickly eating an extra piece of toast. Nathan had known people with sugar imbalance and confronted her.

"I'm worried about you, Alita. You're not taking good care of yourself, and it shows. When was the last time you had Colleen check your blood sugar levels?" he asked forcefully.

"Just before your mother's funeral," she answered without further explanation.

"It's been almost three months. Why haven't you gone to see her?" he asked, observing her carefully for an answer.

She turned away from his penetrating stare, searching for the right words. He leaped from his chair and wrapped his arms around her. "You don't have to answer, Alita. I think I know the reason why. Do you want me to tell you what I think...?"

"All right... all right..." she cried out loud. "I'm having trouble seeing when I drive... Oh, my God, Nathan. I'm afraid I'm going blind!"

It was as he had expected. He knew that she had been studying Braille in the privacy of her apartment.

"My dear lady," he said, holding her in a strong embrace, "You've got to see Colleen as soon as we can get to her. Then you need to go to an eye doctor for corrective glasses. Do not be afraid, my love. We can overcome this situation together. Will you agree for me and Casey to take you to Portland to see Colleen? We can be there by noontime. Would you please call to tell her we're on our way?" she was distraught and clung to him. "Please let me help you. I'll call for you. What's her number?"

She continued to cry on his shoulder. "Her office number is 207-621-2114," she sobbed.

He carried her into the living room and laid her on the couch, placing a pillow under her head. Then he called the number. A secretary answered. He told her who was calling and asked to speak directly to Doctor Atkins, telling her it was important and that he would wait until she was available.

Doctor Atkins answered, "Hello, Nathan. Is anything wrong?"

"Colleen, I'm calling for Alita. Can you take her in for a checkup if I bring her to you? I can be there in an hour's time."

"Yes, of course, Nathan. I had told her that I wanted to see her every two or three weeks. I'm relieved that you'll bring her. By now she probably needs insulin shots, and she must know that too. We can make her feel a lot better. I know that she's a fighter, but she can't fight this battle alone. Is she there with you now?"

"Yes she is," Nathan replied. "We'll be on our way in ten minutes. She's afraid of going blind. Is her diabetes too severe for corrective glasses?"

"The poor girl. I'm angry that she did not turn to me for help sooner. Please tell her that we can correct her vision with diet and dedication. I have a good friend who will make any prescription eye glasses she may need."

"I'll convey that message to her, Colleen. Thanks for easing the worries I had for her. She's a wonderful person whom I intend to marry if she'll have me."

"That's wonderful news to me, old friend. You two deserve each other. Drive carefully. I'll be here when you arrive. Tell my very independent cousin that we both love her very much. Good-bye. Thanks for being there for her, Chief."

An hour and a half later, Doctor Atkins was examining a blood sample from Alita. Casey and Nathan sat quietly in the waiting room.

On the ride to Portland, Nathan had asked Alita to marry him. Casey had smiled at the way his dad was shy asking such an important question. Alita had argued quite forcefully that she would be nothing but a liability to him.

"Diabetes cannot be cured," she cried. "I could be blind..."

Casey's dad was quick to respond, "Well, young lady, we'll just simply deal with whatever comes to us. Between the three of us we can wrestle most any problem to the ground. Is your answer yes?"

"Oh, yes... yes... my wonderful tower of strength. I'll be proud to be your wife...."

In order to fulfill the sacred vows to each other, Nathan wanted to bring to a conclusion three things he had been tentatively contemplating. He shared them with Casey in the waiting room. First, he had a firm offer of $4,500.00 for the house in Belfast. It was a fair price for the property. Next, he had placed five hundred dollars down on the piece of land at the mouth of the Penobscot River. The owner lowered the price to $2,500.00. Now that he and Alita planned to marry, the two of them would have to make the decision to purchase the land and consider what they wanted for a house on the waterfront. Nathan was excited about the possibilities.

"What's the third thing, Dad?" Casey asked.

"You're going to like this one, son. An officer I served with in the Coast Guard has offered me a summer job to take charge of operating a large yacht for private deep sea fishing expeditions from May to October. We'll operate out of Searsport."

Casey thought about what his father had told him. "Can you handle a ship like that, Dad? Could I go on it for a ride?"

"Sure. You're old enough to hire on as a deck hand. You'll have to obey my orders," Nathan joked.

Colleen came out of the examining room and took a seat beside Nathan. "Alita is getting dressed. I want her to see an eye doctor just around the corner from us. She's going to need glasses for everyday use, especially driving. Her reading glasses can also be upgraded. Congratulations on your engagement. Alita is like a little girl, you've made her very happy, Chief. As time goes by for the two of you, you're going to be more and more thankful for choosing my cousin."

"I consider Casey and me two lucky guys. I was scared to death she would refuse my offer of marriage. How is she doing, Doctor Atkins, I've been worried about her for the past few weeks."

"She does have diabetes. I'll supply her with the equipment and medication she needs. She's a wonderful nurse, and I'm sure she'll take good care of herself. She'll be able to continue with her everyday activities in moderation, but she should avoid stress. You can help a lot by seeing that she eats something every two hours. When out shopping or on a trip, she should get in the habit of carrying food with her. Crackers and cheese or peanut butter are excellent snack between meals. Fruits of all kinds are also good. Alita's system, in particular, her pancreas has stopped producing insulin. We've got to replace that important substance in her body and regulate its amount. I've given her some literature you and Casey should read." Doctor Atkins turned to Casey. "You're growing into a fine young man like your dad. You take good care of him and his soon-to-be bride." She warmly embraced him.

Shy with the public display of affection, Casey answered, "I promise, Doctor Atkins."

"I'm relieved that you've seen her, Colleen. I can rest easier now. Your cousin has given new meaning to my life in the short time that I've known her. I have much to be thankful for," he said, embracing Doctor Atkins.

Alita walked out of the examination room with a renewed confidence and a lighter step. She radiated contentment and ran into Nathan's arms with tears of happiness flowing across her cheeks.

They immediately went to the eye doctor where she was measured for glasses. The doctor told her he would have her glasses completed in an hour. It was early afternoon so they went to a restaurant for fried clams and fish chowder.

Later, Alita came out of the eye doctor's office wearing her new glasses. She claimed that she was able to see better than ever and asked Nathan if she could drive the Studebaker. Eager to please, he opened the driver door for her.

"Now, my dear fiancée, I have a surprise for you. Do you mind if we take a trip up Route One past Belfast? I have something I want you to see.'

"Are you going to tell me what the surprise is?" she asked. He and Casey saw the impish side of Alita once again, and were thankful.

"Only that it has to do with our future. And I'll say no more on the subject. Now you get us out of the city onto Route One North."

Two hours later, he directed Alita to the narrow roadway leading to the parcel of land, asking her to pull the Studebaker right to the edge of the water and stop. Then he told her about selling the old family home and the prospects of building on the site where the Studebaker was parked. He also mentioned the offer of summer employment doing fishing expeditions, and when he finally got his degree in forestry, he would like to start a consulting forest management business in southern Maine. Many large forest holdings were held by absentee owners who needed the services of a professional forester. Combining forestry with a part time job on the water was like a dream come true for him. She shared his enthusiasm.

Alita climbed out of the car and breathed deeply of the fresh cool sea air. She looked in every direction, but was pulled like a magnet to the east with the dark blue waters of the Atlantic laced with small islands in the far distance. The place had an energy and a power that she could feel. Slowly she turned to Nathan who was waiting behind her in anticipation of her reply. Before she spoke, he knew what her answer would be. Captivated by the serenity and peace, small tears welled in the corner of her eyes.

"Oh, Nathan, this location could be our piece of Heaven-on-earth!" she cried, leaping into his waiting arms.

Together they looked to the future, embracing tomorrow.

THE END

Other Historical Romance Novels

BY

Clifton LaBree

A Song for Lisa   A Historical Romance

This is the story of a young American woman captured by the Japanese in the Philippines, 1941. Like most prisoners, she was brutalized and sadistically treated with a cruel disregard for human life. Three years later, Lisa and her companions had reached the low point of starvation and abuse .....

Lake of Three Sorrows   A Historical Romance

A warm spiritually uplifting story of courage, commitment, and sacrifice. This is the story of Dale Cooper, a battle-weary American soldier who served in two world wars.

Flickering Flame (Colonial Series Book One)

A historical novel, about the Cullen family who settled in Portsmouth, New Hampshire, and their participation in events prior to the French and Indian War. Freedom and opportunity were on the march, but it extracted a heavy price. Frontier settlers were ruthlessly killed and butchered by rampaging Indians lead by French officers and Jesuit priests who frequently incited them to greater levels of inhumanity...

Raising the Torch (Colonial Series Book Two)

A continuation of the saga from Flickering Flame, Colonial Series book one, of the Cullen family in Colonial Portsmouth. This is a moving story of love and sacrifice when a small colony had the audacity to fight for independence from their motherland...

Non-Fiction Books

By

Clifton LaBree

New Hampshire's General John Stark, Live Free or Die: Death Is Not the Greatest of Evils

Publisher - Fading Shadows Imprint

A fresh look at one of America's staunchest defenders of liberty and freedom. John Stark was a courageous New Hampshire citizen-soldier who fought in both, the French and Indian War, and the Revolutionary War. His pursuit of leadership excellence on the battlefield distinguished him as one of the most successful combat commanders of the war, and one of the least appreciated.

His selflessness, modest life style, and devotion to the cause of freedom are an inspiration that time has not diminished. He remains today the embodiment of the frugal, independent, and cantankerous New Hampshire Yankee.

Gentle Warrior, General Oliver Prince Smith, USMC

Published by - Kent State University Press. Kent, Ohio, 2001

The Story of one of the United States Marine Corps best General Officer. His flawless performance in Korea is a story that needed to be told.

About: FADING SHADOWS IMPRINT

Fading Shadows Imprint was established to bring to the public books of historical events and portraits of people enduring tragic circumstances of by-gone days. Hopefully, they will generate a deep appreciation and respect for the exceptionalness of the United States of America, and an appreciation for the sacrifice and selflessness of those who valiantly served for liberty and freedom.

The characters are fictional, but the historical events and dates have been seriously researched and are factually presented. Some books feature incidents during the French and Indian Wars as well as the War for Independence.

World Wars I and II are eras rich in stories that beg to be told. I've tried to pay tribute to the collective courage and heroism, often unheralded, that has defined Americans in every engagement. It was a time when the immortality of dreams and aspirations were defended by the blood of young men and women. There is a beautiful monument and cemetery in a small French village where thousands of white crosses and Stars-of-David are set in perfect alignment, honoring thousands of American soldiers who gave their last full measure. A large granite slab bearing mute witness to their sacrifice has the following words chiseled in stone: TIME WILL NOT DIM THE GLORY OF THEIR DEEDS. Another monument reads: VIRTUE AND COURAGE ARE THEIR OWN MONUMENT AND REWARD. Those simple words define the American soldier from the dark days of the Revolutionary War to the present. They are an American treasure, unique in the history of the world.

Every generation has its own signature and characteristics that uniquely define them. The World War II generation is defined by the immortality of the ideals and truth they gallantly defended.

The United States has freely given precious blood and treasure to defend the rights of man to be free, and we have never asked for anything in return. No other nation on the planet has sacrificed so much for the noble virtues of liberty and freedom. We hope that the selections offered by Fading Shadows Imprint will touch your hearts and generate a deeper appreciation and love for our country.

www.ingramcontent.com/pod-product-compliance
Lightning Source LLC
Chambersburg PA
CBHW072123170626
46813CB00004B/1675